Pious Poison

A JESSAMY WARD MYSTERY

PENELOPE CRESS, STEVE HIGGS

Contents

All The Single Ladies

"I am all in pain. My heart will never mend."

"Of course it will, Frederico. I understand my sister has a certain charm but you... Look, see how the membership of the Wesberrey 'Walkers' has flourished since you took over. All these ladies, eager to get fit because of you."

In truth, most of the 'Walkers' were more interested in flirting with the tanned, athletic Adonis who chased my sister halfway across the world than any exercise regime.

"And they are all beautiful women, but they are not my Zuzu. She was my... How do you say? Soul mate. Yes?"

"Is there such a thing?" I looked over the shoulder of the lovesick Brazilian and cast my gaze in the harbour's direction and the mainland beyond. The poor man. He travelled halfway across the world to propose to my sister, only to find her romantically interested in a modern-day Errol Flynn lookalike. I understood his pain. I had once foolishly thought that my sister's latest conquest, Inspector Lovington, had a romantic interest in me. Now here we both were, Frederico and I, two neon-clad cast-offs, sipping mediocre filtered coffee together, whilst the golden couple were enjoying the joy-filled rush of a new relationship. I had accepted the situation, really I had. But I was afraid that Frederico still believed Zuzu would come to her senses and run back to him. I knew my sister. Once she moved on, she never looked back. "Let's talk about something else. You have your interview at Stourchester University soon. Are you prepared?"

It turned out that Frederico was a highly regarded primatologist. My sister had joined him to help his research on the lives and times of a colony of endangered monkeys comically known as buffy-headed marmosets. I was still unclear why she had abandoned him to return to Wesberrey. She had never felt it necessary to explain to me what had happened or, more tragically, to the poor wreck now sitting in front of me crying into his coffee at the window table of the island's only pub, the 'Cat and Fiddle'. He was a long way from home.

"Stourchester will not be a challenge. My research and academic record speak for me. What will be a challenge is working in such an institution. Their animal science programmes are very, how can I put this? Unambitious. I will be here, near her, and working. But, is it always this cold?"

"This is England! We were very lucky to have the spring sun this morning for our walk. Last week we were dodging hailstones, remember?"

He laughed. I knew it was genuine because it split his face in two, his whole lower face replaced by a bandana of pearly whites.

Most of the other lady members of the 'Wesberrey Walkers' had splintered off from us when we arrived at the pub. It was an interesting ritual they had adopted. Whereas I was happy to crash with my order of a large filter coffee and a packet of cheese and onion crisps, the moment we stepped inside the pub they all headed to the ladies' toilet to refresh, rejuvenate, and re-plump their makeup before joining us. It was amusing to see their not-very-subtle attempts to get Frederico's attention. They could all sit here naked, though I doubt he would notice.

It was my effervescent parish secretary, Barbara Graham, who had convinced me to join her in the Wesberrey 'Walkers' shortly after I joined the parish nearly two months ago. Then, when Frederico arrived last month and seemed determined to stay, despite my sister's attention having migrated elsewhere, I invited him to come along. As there were no cars on the island, people's lives were far from sedentary. Being a tourist destination, with a small native population, most sporting activities happened during the 'season' from Easter through to the end of October. In the way of keep-fit pastimes, Wesberrey's 'Walkers' was the best I could offer — a raggedy bunch of middle-aged dumplings dressed in neon lycra and eighties-style leg warmers. By the end of the first walk, Frederico had agreed to take over the group with a promise to whip us all into shape. Since then he had added two mid-week evening exercise sessions in the church hall besides the regular weekend walk.

Barbara was one of the first to emerge from the toilets but she made a sure and certain beeline to the bar where she knew she would find Phil Vickers, the twinkling-eyed verger of St. Bridget's Abbey church and owner of the 'Cat and Fiddle'. Phil was a master of many trades and the only object of Barbara's desire. I had grown accustomed to their flirtatious banter but was still unsure of the status of their relationship. All I knew was Barbara was uninterested in my Brazilian friend. I could not say the same for the group that emerged from the toilets next.

"Reverend, budge up. Can't have you keeping this hunk of a man to yourself!"

"Now, now, Verity, you are making him blush. You must excuse my sister, Frederico. She becomes a giggling schoolgirl at the sight of a handsome face. You should have seen her last Tuesday when the Chief Inspector came into the salon for a quick trim. I believe he was meeting your sister, Reverend. Now there's a man with a strong upper lip."

"Ssshh, Avril." Verity looked at her twin with a disapproving stare. "You know poor Freddy here still carries a torch for the Reverend's sister. But Freddy, you mustn't pine. Plenty more fish in the sea. If you ask me, she's mad to choose the dishy Inspector over you." Verity leaned across the table and cupped Frederico's hand in hers. "Oh, he has a certain English charm, but his pencil moustache is nothing compared to your healthy PI Magnum affair. May I ask how you keep it looking so glossy?"

Avril shoved her sister with her right elbow. "Glossy! He's not a prize-winning dog. I am so sorry, Frederico. Verity is obsessed with masculine facial hair."

"Please, ladies. I am, erm, honoured by your kind words but ... Jess, I will go to my room now. If you will excuse me? I have to prepare for my interview." Frederico stood up, and bowing his apologies, made as quick an exit as possible to his temporary accommodation above the pub.

"See, Avril, you scared him off." Verity harrumphed. "Go to the bar and get me a Gin Fizz and some crisps, see if they have any pork scratchings, and bring over a menu. I'm famished." Avril held out her hand expectedly, indicating that this trip to the bar would cost her twin dearly. Verity huffed her way through the contents of her 'genuine replica' pink padded Chanel bag with a gold chain, eventually producing a twenty pound note which she crumpled into her sister's waiting palm. "And make that gin a double."

"That's a nice bag." I ventured though I thought it was a little garish.

"Yeah, I picked it up two years ago on holiday in Turkey. In the Grand Bazaar. It was a bargain. I bartered it down. They expect that, don't they? I think the guy on the stall fancied me. Very charming, aren't they? The Turks. Avril wants to go back this summer, but I was thinking of trying Cape Verde." Without so much as a beat, Verity changed her focus from me to another 'Walker' who had just emerged from the toilet. "Whoo-hoo! Audrey! Come over and join us. We're gonna get some lunch, aren't we, Reverend? Don't need to hold our stomachs in now that Freddy has retired to his room, eh?"

Audrey Matthews was the secretary of the local primary school, and most of our encounters were frosty. I seemed to have upset her somehow when I first arrived. Despite several efforts on my part to build bridges, our relationship remained as cold as ever.

"Vicar, Verity, I'm sorry but I need to get home to look after the shop. Poor Stan was stressed out with a delivery this morning, and I promised I'd head back straightaway and relieve him." Her husband Stan was the proprietor of the hardware shop, 'Bits 'n' Pieces', on the other side of Market Square. "Maybe next Saturday. Or, if I can convince our lad to mind the shop, perhaps I can bring Stan to join us. Lord knows he needs the exercise more than I do."

"Well, never mind." Verity pulled a clownishly sad face. "Still all set to do your nails on Wednesday?" Audrey nodded, smiled politely, and walked away. She bumped into Avril as she crossed the face of the bar, causing a tiny bit of pink gin to spill over Avril's blouse. Worried she might lose the rest of her hard-won drink, Verity tried to take charge.

"Avril, you clumsy mare! Give 'em to me."

"I'm perfectly capable." Avril dodged her sister's hand and set the drinks down on the wooden table. She pulled out the menus from under her arm and threw them in front of us. "And you can go up to order the food. I'm not your skivvy."

I knew how annoying sisters can be; I had two of my own, but Verity and Avril took sibling rivalry to a higher level. Lunch was a veritable feast of cutting remarks, put-downs and sarcastic humour, at the opposite twin's expense. The other members of the 'Wesberrey Walkers'" were wise to keep their distance. On several occasions, I cast a desperate look over to Barbara and Phil to come and rescue me. Or to Martha, the wise and uber-efficient hospital receptionist who had positioned herself at the opposite table with the other 'Walkers'. I couldn't attract their attention because they had their backs to me. The other 'Walkers' seated at the table included a married couple, Judith and Keith Hudson, and Mandy McGuire. Mandy's brother Bob ran the local ferry.

Eventually the twins' jibes about each other morphed into jibes about our rival walking groups.

Avril started. "Reverend, are you looking forward to the annual Wesberrey Walkathon on Easter Saturday? I think with the training regime that Freddy has us all under now, we stand a brilliant chance of keeping the trophy on the Island this year. Don't you?"

The Wesberrey Walkathon is the primary reason the 'Walkers' were set up. The yearly event covers an eight-mile circuit of the island with prizes for completing three distance stages: eight, sixteen, and thirty-two miles. Competitors who successfully complete the full thirty-two-mile walk are entered automatically into a speed trial, and the fastest time wins the coveted Wesberrey Walkathon Cup.

"Yeah, I can't wait to wipe the smug look off of the 'Otters'. They think they are so much better than we are..." Verity spat out the word 'Otters' with much venom.

"The 'Otters'?" I asked.

"Yes, the Oysterhaven Town Ramblers Association O.T.R.A. - 'Otters'. They are so up themselves with their hiking boots and those upside-down maps in plastic bags they hang from their necks. They have compasses and everything. Pointless in the 'Walkathon', we only go on the main roads. You can't get lost on Wesberrey." Avril delighted in telling me more about the great rivalry between the 'Walkers', the 'Otters' and the Stourchester 'Strollers'. It seems it has been going on for over a decade. "But this year, nothing's gonna stop us winning. There are more of us, and we have Frederico. He's our secret weapon."

"Secret weapon?" I wondered if Verity was being a tad over dramatic. "Do we really need one?"

"Hush now, Reverend. You'll find out soon enough."

Back To Work

"Martha, are you on shift this afternoon? I could give you a lift on 'Cilla' if you like?"

As she straddled the seat behind me, I handed Martha my spare scooter helmet and off we set for the Cottage Hospital. 'Cilla', my burnt orange Lambretta, had revolutionised my ability to shoot across the island spreading God's message. I couldn't imagine how I would manage without her.

"Tank you, Reverend, dat would be a great kindness. I'm not sure these ole knees would manage the climb up Abbey Road Drive, not after dat workout."

"Or the raspberry and apple crumble I saw you eating."

"Hehe, true dat!" Martha wrapped her bingo-winged arms around my waist and linked her fingers. "Hehe, looks like yuh've had your share of crumble as well, Vicar!"

We both laughed.

Much as I loved whizzing across the island like a clerical bumble bee, *buzz buzz*, it had meant I was walking less though, and I sympathised with Martha about Frederico's new regime. I'm sure it was effective, but boy, did we feel the burn.

I dropped Martha off at the end of the road. The hospital is next to the vicarage, and I wanted to dash home quickly to put on my clerical collar before my rounds. The hospital only had a few patients at the moment, so I had a bit of time.

"Mummy, Jess is back!" Zuzu poked her head around the kitchen door at the end of the hall and called in to my mother. For the past few months, my new home had been host to most of my family. Zuzu and my mother had been staying since before my induction, then my sister Rosie with her son Luke arrived fleeing a cheating husband and quite aggressive bailiffs. We had quickly adapted to the new living arrangements, but sometimes I admit I missed the peace of my former life. I craved the alone time I used to take for granted.

"I'm not stopping. Just grabbing this..." I reached into a bowl on the hall stand.

My mother emerged from the kitchen doorway, drying her wet hands with a checked dishcloth.

"Jessamy, I appreciate you are busy, but we need to talk about the wills. I have invited Tom and Ernest for dinner. I thought we could explore our options with Ernest... informally."

Ernest was a semi-retired solicitor charged with overseeing the estates of the late Violet Smith and the related trust funds of Lord Somerstone, both bequeathing not insubstantial sums and assets to myself and my sisters. Tom and Ernest were also our nearest neighbours. They lived together in the 'White House' overlooking the cliffs. Between them they ran the 'Cliff Railway' (a funicular train that linked the top of the cliffs with the harbour below). Their volunteering portfolio also extended to their being my churchwardens. I had been meaning to ask them to dinner since I moved in, but events just got the better of me.

"That sounds a wonderful idea, Mum. Catch up later." I snatched my collar from its resting place and made my escape.

***

"So, tell me more about the rivalry between the 'Walkers' and the 'Otters'?"

8

As had become our weekly habit, Sam and I had returned to her office for some tea and a natter after my Saturday rounds. Sam had been my best friend at school before my family left the island for life in the city, first Stourchester, and eventually London. At which point Sam and I lost touch. My fault really, as I wasn't much of a pen pal.

"Hmmm, well... I would have thought your parish councillors would have brought you up to speed by now. What is it? Two, three weeks away?" Sam leaned across and plucked a tissue from the box on her desk to wipe the crumbs of her sausage roll from the corners of her mouth. "I mean, it's one of the premier events of the Wesberrey social calendar. It marks the beginning of the season and all that jazz."

"I think it is on the agenda for Wednesday's meeting. That's if I survive Tuesday's 'Walkers' Workout. Frederico is a harsh taskmaster. You should join us!"

"What, and give up flaky baked goods?" Sam recoiled in horror as she stuffed the last bite of sausage meat wrapped in puff pastry in her mouth. "What has he got you eating? Looks like air to me."

"I ate at the 'Cat and Fiddle'."

"Well, I don't do organised communal torture, and especially not if it involves lycra." Not that Sam had to worry, she had always been naturally lithe. "How is poor Frederico? Still pining over your sister?"

"I'm afraid so." I nodded into my near-empty cup of tea. "Any more in that pot?" Sam shook the teapot and indicated that I should scooch over for a refill. "He seems determined to stay here until she changes her mind. I have tried to tell him Zuzu never goes back and certainly not now. She has Inspector Dave wrapped around her little finger. The other evening, Dave was talking about buying one of the new houses up on School Lane, or an apartment overlooking the marina at Oysterhaven, so he can be based nearer."

"Surely Oysterhaven makes more sense for work, though it's still quite the commute to Stourchester."

"Sam, that isn't the point! He is thinking of moving to be nearer to Zuzu! It's only been a few weeks. He's acting like a love-sick puppy. How does she do it, eh? Two gorgeous, intelligent men ready to turn their own lives upside down to be with her."

"Ah, I knew it! You do think Frederico is attractive."

"I'm a vicar, not a nun!"

"So..."

"So what? Look, the man has travelled across the world to declare his love for a heavenly, fair-haired goddess. He is not going to shift his affections to her plump, mousy-haired sister! Anyway, didn't we agree I don't need a man? And we were right, I don't. So stop trying to match make. Frederico needs a good friend, someone he can talk to, and that's my job. Okay?"

"Okay." Sam sighed. "So what do you want to know about the annual bun fight that is the 'Walkathon'?"

The Dinner Party

T om and Ernest arrived promptly at 7.30 pm and Mum, as expected, was more than ready for our little soirée.

"Gentlemen, let me take your things. It's blowing up quite a storm out there. So good of you to venture out on a night like this." Mum fussed around our elderly guests, making a point of hanging each of their coats, hats and scarves on individual hooks on the mahogany hall stand. We had all been made to remove our paraphernalia from the stand before they arrived.

"Oh, we wouldn't have missed it for the world!" Tom was always the most excitable of the pair. "We are only a hop, skip, and a jump away. Hardly worth putting our coats on, to be honest."

Tom held out his hand to Ernest as they walked through the hall. Ernest's hand remained at his side, his mind focussed on other things. "Thank you for the invitation, Mrs Ward. Tom is the cook in our house, so I think he is relishing a night off." Ernest's usual stern profile softened as he looked at his partner. I had often mused at the simple and obvious connection they had. They just perfected each other. "Though I hope you haven't gone to too much trouble, Mrs Ward."

"Please, call me Beverley. And you have met my daughters..."

Tom eagerly stepped forward and confirmed each of our identities with a flamboyant flourish of his hand. "We know the Reverend. She looks just like you, around the eyes and your eldest, Zuzu. Now, she is definitely her father's child, again, the eyes." Tom looked wistfully towards the ceiling. "I remember Michael Ward had the most penetrating blue stare. Quite a knee-trembler." Then his soft misty gaze fell on my younger sister. "Ah, Rosie, by name and complexion. Mrs Ward, you could be twins!"

"I am quite happy being her mother." Mum was not easily flattered. "We usually eat in the kitchen, but I thought it would be nice to break out the vicarage silverware and make use of that stunning regency dining room. This way, gentlemen."

There was a lot of mahogany furniture in the vicarage, all dating from when the house was built. The dining room, though, held the most daintily turned table and chairs. The table was now ornamented with sparkly crystal glasses, vases, and silver candlesticks. There were eight place settings. A small army of silver cutlery guarded each pile of porcelain flatware on three sides. Mum had even put out name placers to ensure we sat in the correct gender order. Luke, Mum, Ernest and Zuzu on the far side and directly opposite me, Tom, Rosie and... I reached out to pick up the mystery name card.

"Frederico!"

"Yes, poor lamb. I feel bad for him stuck above that pub morning, noon and night."

Zuzu looked like she was about to explode. "Mummy! You invited Freddy! And you didn't think to ask if that was okay with me at all?"

"Well, Susannah. He's *my* guest." My mother always reverted to Zuzu's birth name when she was angry with her. "We needed another man to make up the numbers. If you cannot even be civil after he has travelled all this way then..."

"But why did you have to sit him opposite me?" Zuzu moved the name placers around. "Here, I've swapped him with Luke. Jessie, you can babysit Freddy."

As if on cue, the doorbell rang.

"Gentlemen, I am so sorry, if you could please take your seats. I will let in our other guest."

Mum scurried out into the hallway, and the rest of the bewildered party sat themselves down. I tried to catch my eldest sibling's eye so I could glare my embarrassment and disapproval at her, but she was furiously occupying herself with a linen napkin.

Frederico entered the room dressed in a light grey, single-breasted Italian suit that emphasised the broadness of his shoulders and the narrowness of his waist. Underneath, he had a matching waistcoat overlaying a crisp white shirt and a stunning pink tie. In his hands he carried four red roses which he gallantly handed out to my mother and sisters before walking around to the end of the table where I sat, laying my rose across my top plate. He bowed to the group and sat down.

It was quite an entrance and one that certainly impressed Tom, if not my sister, Zuzu. Tom shoved out his hand towards our latest addition.

"Hi, Frederico D'Souza, I believe. I don't think we have been properly introduced. I'm Tom Jennings and this handsome devil is Ernest Woodward. I understand that you are from Brazil. How exotic! What made you come here to dreary Wesberrey?"

Frederico shook Tom's hand and nodded at Ernest. Casting a hopeful eye down the line at my sister, he answered with one word.

"Amor."

***

Both Zuzu and Frederico acted reserved for most of the dinner, speaking only to acknowledge the deliciousness of the food before them or to respond politely to questions from their immediate neighbours. I wondered what my mother had hoped to achieve with this strange gathering. Fortunately, our other two guests were well mannered and worldly enough to take charge over most of the conversation, diplomatically navigating a safe course through funny anecdotes and small talk until it was time for dessert. Finally, over delicate white plates, each featuring a trio of miniature desserts (raspberry meringue, vanilla cheesecake topped with a raspberry coulis and chocolate brownie with raspberry sauce), Mum started the conversation about the wills.

"So, Ernest, how do we set about refusing that money?"

Ernest looked circumspectly down the table. "Is that what you all want to do? It's a fairly simple procedure. I just need to draft a deed of variation for you all to sign, and the funds and other assets will revert to the estate or to a beneficiary of your choice. But all the current beneficiaries must be in agreement."

"Mummy, is that why you invited Freddy here this evening? Did you think I would cow down rather than argue with you in front of my ex-lover? This is outrageous! I understand you had a personal beef with Violet Smith and Lord S, but we need that money. Rosie has lost everything. What about Luke? What about me? Or your granddaughters? Freya's at university getting into a ton of debt just to get an education. This money, these assets... well... I understand they can't bring Dad back. But it was over forty years ago! He's dead, Violet is dead, Geoffrey Somerstone is dead, but we are all still very much alive."

"It's blood money, Zuzu. The proceeds of two guilty consciences. Nothing good can come from taking this money. They killed your father!" My mother's voice quivered with forty years of rage.

"No. He killed himself."

We all turned to look at Rosie.

"We were there. I remember. Mum, you wrapped me up in a blanket, and we chased him up to Love Lane. It was so dark, and I kept stumbling. I slowed you down. We saw that wild woman with the black hair, like snakes on her head. She was screaming. All crazy. Dad was running away from her. But she caught him. In front of the wall here. The one outside the vicarage. You made me hide behind the hedge and keep my head down. But I could see they were fighting. She was crying and trying to put his hand on her belly."

"Rosie, sweetheart. You don't have to say anymore." My mother crumpled in her seat.

"Mum, you were there? You took Rosie?" I gasped. I thought I knew all my family's tragic secrets, but Rosie was there! Little Rosie, my sweet little sister.

"Please, let me finish." Rosie raised her bowed head. Her eyes were red-rimmed, full of tears waiting for permission to flow. I looked at Zuzu, and we both nodded. We knew, that no matter how painful to hear, Rosie needed to tell us what had happened. "Dad pulled his hand back and ran to the cliff edge. That woman ran after him. Mum shouted, 'Michael. Stop!' Dad looked back. He stood there. He just stood there looking at Mum, shaking his head. Then he turned toward the cliffs. I didn't see him again."

Silence. No one knew what to say.

Mum rallied herself and cleared away the plates. "Gentleman, I'm sure you don't mind if we call it an early night. I hope you've enjoyed your meal."

Tom, Ernest, and Frederico didn't need asking twice. Their sense of relief at being able to make a dignified getaway was palpable. Ernest spoke on their behalf.

"I think it is customary for the gentlemen to retire for a cigar and a glass of whiskey. Mr D'Souza, would you care to join us at the White House? Tom and I rarely have company and yet we have a fine collection of malts." Frederico bowed his head in affirmation, and the three men thanked us kindly for the hospitality, my mother for a wonderful feast and were back outside in the whirling storm in record time.

I think it devastated Luke that he couldn't find an excuse to join them. Instead, the gloomy teenager moved chairs and wrapped his arms around his weeping mother.

"Dad committed suicide." Zuzu stabbed her fork into what remained of her chocolate brownie. "He killed himself. He saw you and just threw himself to his death. The selfish bastard!"

"Susannah! That's no way to talk about your father!" Mum looked as if the last forty years had all rushed to age her in one sitting. I saw, for the first time, that she was a frail woman in her seventies. All the pain of her life showed in her posture, her skin, her eyes.

"Tell me how he wasn't selfish, eh? He was carrying on with any woman he could find. The entire island knew. I heard rumours even at primary school. He thought he had made Violet Smith pregnant. Yet he abandoned her. He abandoned you. He abandoned us! He was selfish and weak. And in front of Rosie?"

"He didn't see me. I was good at hiding. And it was dark and..."

Zuzu turned on my mother.

"Why did you take her with you? Why did you even follow him? What, to beg and plead for him to come back? The lying, cheating bastard. You'd have taken him back, wouldn't you? You always did. I heard the rows. The walk up the gravel path, the gate closing. He always did what he wanted to do. You couldn't stop him. You couldn't save him!"

"I loved him."

"Bah! Love! Men are all the same. They only want the chase. Look at Freddy. I treat him like dirt, and he follows me across the planet. But if I let him put that ring on my finger, he would be off thinking about his next conquest or staking out some endangered mammals somewhere. Selfish, the lot of them."

"Zuzu, I don't think that's fair." I tried to reason with my sister. I refused to believe all men were the same. I truly believed that Frederico was a gentle, kind man.

"Well, what about Teddy? Luke, sorry to bad-mouth your father, but he ran off with his secretary, and it wasn't his first affair. Freddy, Teddy. They are all the same!"

"Zuzu, you're upset and lashing out. They aren't the same, and you know it. There are plenty of honourable men in this world. Plenty of loving, faithful men. Look at Tom and Ernest."

"Yes, and they're gay! The best ones always are!" Zuzu threw her fork across the table.

Sensing a need to move the conversation on, I thought I would do what any British vicar would do in such circumstances.

"Right! Well, Mum, you look like you need a good strong cup of tea. Rosie, Luke. Let's all move into the morning room, and I'll put on the kettle. Zuzu, you finish clearing up and help me load the dishwasher. Let's just have a bit of calm. We can talk about it again later. Okay?"

It worked. Tea is a miracle in a cup.

Mothering Sunday

None of us said much that evening. What else was there to say? Rosie's disclosure blew apart everything we all thought we knew about the past four decades and reformed it like that robot thing in Terminator. My father was still dead, except now we all knew what had happened. Did it change anything? Not really. He had left us, and we were still there to support each other. The revelation did, however, help my mother reconsider her objections to the money. She remained unhappy, but there was no escaping that we could use it. Especially Rosie, who had lost everything - her husband, her home and her business.

Breakfast the next day was tense. It was Mother's Day, and we had agreed beforehand to treat Mum to a cooked breakfast in bed, which meant rising extra early to beat her to the kitchen. The upside of this early start was that it gave the three of us some time to talk about the night before over the distracting business of cooking eggs and making toast.

Mum hated any kind of fuss, thankfully. She received breakfast with love but with no expectation that we would sit and watch her eat. After a quick exchange of cards, flowers and hugs the three of us left Mum in peace to get on with her morning.

Hugely relieved, I moved on to my next pressing deadline. Mass was in two hours and I didn't have a sermon.

As it was 'Mothering Sunday' I knew, at least, what the theme would be. Whilst in Britain this religious event had now morphed into Hallmark's idea of 'Mother's Day', the original Mothering Sunday had no connection to mothers at all. The word 'mothering' referred to the 'mother church'. On the fourth Sunday of Lent, people would return to their family church for a special service. 'Going a-mothering' became a special holiday where domestic servants traditionally had the day off to visit their families. Mothering Sunday also falls close to the feast of the Annunciation, the Church's official marking of the conception of our Lord. Another celebration of motherhood and the gift of life. It also falls in the middle of our lead up to Easter, and each year Lent gives us the gift of a fresh start. Reflecting on the events of the previous evening, I thought I would write something about the importance of forgiveness, returning to the loving embrace of your mother, and the ever-present hope of starting over.

Armed with a coffee strong enough to stand my spoon up in, I powered up the electronic beast that dominated my mahogany desk. The computer was old and with the addition of Luke's games, now terribly slow. Still, the cogs whirred, and when it awoke, a series of bleeps told me there were several emails in my inbox. Just a quick look. I know I had this sermon to write, but it could be an invitation to lunch from Keanu Reeves. I mean, it would be just wrong to keep him waiting for a reply.

Sadly, there was no email from Keanu. But there was an intriguing one from Reverend Richard Cattermole, the vicar of St. Mildred's in Oysterhaven, reminding me he and a small delegation from both the Oysterhaven Town Ramblers Association and the Stourchester 'Strollers' were visiting on Tuesday to work through the arrangements for the 'Walkathon'. With everything I'd heard, I knew I needed to conduct these tense negotiations with the utmost tact and diplomacy - lest the three walking groups incited an international incident that would end life as we know it. So, I carefully worded my reply:

No worries, Richard. Looking forward to meeting you on Tuesday for a spot of lunch. I am sure Barbara will delight us with one of her famous cakes.

Best,

Jessamy.

A Slice of Cake, Vicar

B arbara did an amazing job with the catering. I think there was an element of pride at stake because the selection was vast, and from the bags beneath her eyes, I suspected that my secretary had been up all night ensuring we had this magnificent spread. In the interests of healthy eating, she had made most of the cakes from non-dairy, fat-free recipes and natural sources of sugar. There was even a bowl of salad and a collection of vegetable crudités with assorted dips.

I had to comment on the delicious spread. "Barbara, you never fail in surprising me with your culinary prowess. You really should think about entering the 'Bake Off'!"

"Oh, you are sweet, Vicar, but I'm a bit worried I've made too much. You never know how many people have given up cakes and sweets for Lent. I won't be touching any myself. No sugar for me!"

As the small crowd descended onto the sweet treats, I assured her that there was no need to worry. There were a few protests about sticking to their Lenten vows, but there was still more hummus than cake left after we filled our plates.

Several 'Walkers' were present. Verity and Avril deemed this meeting important enough to leave their junior stylists in charge of the salon, and Judith had left her husband Keith running her market stall. She also brought an array of edible treats. Judith had a small business making homemade jams and preserves, a range cunningly titled 'Hudson's Homemade'.

The kaleidoscopic collection of her wares lined the back of the trestle table. There were jams and chutneys in every hue from damson and plum through to an intriguing jar with three different layers of raspberry, peach, and kiwi to represent traffic lights.

"What a clever idea - Traffic Jam! These all look so pretty," I said, picking up a dusky pink jar labelled 'Rhubarb and Vanilla'. "I've never had rhubarb jam before, though I love a crumble and custard…"

"Please, take it, Vicar. I rarely sell too many rhubarb varieties. Which is a shame as it makes a lovely jam. But this year they are selling like hot cakes! I bring a selection along every year, discounted prices as a peace offering." Judith leaned in conspiratorially. "Though such gestures are wasted on the 'Otters'. They like to lord it over us every year, especially my cousin, Maureen."

"Maureen?"

"Yes, the one in the green." Trying not to make it too obvious, I searched the room. I should have spotted the resemblance straight away. Maureen and Judith looked more like twins than Verity and Avril did. Both Judith and Maureen stood with arched shoulders, each so thin I could count the bones revealed in the décolletage above their matching white tee shirts. The main difference in their appearance came from Maureen sporting an emerald green cardigan and Judith preferring to wear a cobalt blue version. Each cousin wore their greying hair short. Both wore blue denim jeans and white trainers.

"I can see the family resemblance. So, your cousin lives in Oysterhaven?"

"Yes, she has a farm there. It's where I get most of the ingredients for my preserves. I am hoping she's brought some fresh rhubarb with her today. I made this batch with the beautiful forced stalks she brought over last week to market. Such a gorgeous colour. Did you know they grow them in the dark and harvest by candlelight? You can hear the stems growing. Quite magical, don't you think? That there's the last jar, Vicar."

"Well, thank you for letting me have this then. I will look forward to spreading it on my toast in the morning."

It was just as well there was so much choice, as the 'small delegation' turned out to be over half a dozen members representing both our rival groups. Once everyone had loaded up their plates with goodies, we sat facing each other across a large circle of chairs in the centre of the hall. On the opposing side sat Reverend Cattermole and three other 'Otters', including Maureen. The 'Otters' were flanked by a further four 'Strollers' each one wearing matching electric blue sweatshirts with the word 'Strollers' in white appliqué across their chests. The 'Strollers' also seemed to have matching grey jogging bottoms, but that may have just been a coincidence.

Balancing a plate piled high with a rainbow selection of Barbara's cakes, Reverend Cattermole kicked off proceedings. "Reverend Ward, I don't know how much you know about the history of the Wesberrey Walkathon, but it has become the highlight of the county's walking calendar. The 'Otters' have won the challenge for the past seven years." Reverend Cattermole was more portly than I imagined the chair of the Oysterhaven ramblers to be. At least he appreciated Barbara's efforts in the kitchen, some of the remains of which he was now dusting off his shirt.

"So I understand, and before that, Stourchester 'Strollers' held the crown. Wesberrey, sadly, has always come third." With a little snigger to myself, I added, "but we plan to give you both a run, or rather a walk, for your money this year."

Well, at least I laughed at my joke. No one else seemed to find it amusing.

"The Walkathon is no laughing matter, Reverend Ward." Maureen had a voice as razor-like as her bone structure.

"Perhaps we should start over?" I offered. "Maybe we should all introduce ourselves?"

"I'll go first." One of the Stourchester blue sweatshirts raised her hand. "I'm Sonia, Sonia Hampton, and I'm a student at the University. Professor Linden encouraged me to join."

"I shall go next then." A slender lady with rather flat features and an ironed straight, jaw-length bob shuffled in her seat. "I'm Helen Linden."

"Traitor!"

We all turned to a beige jumper and tweed skirt sitting next to Reverend Cattermole.

"Eunice! Please, Helen moved to the 'Strollers' because of work pressures. I am sure we can still hold our own this year without her." Reverend Cattermole reassured his team.

The beige jumper harrumphed in her seat. "Well, if we lose this year, we shall all know who to blame. My name is Eunice Drinkwater, Secretary of the Oysterhaven Ramblers Association."

"And I'm Conrad Beckworth, treasurer. I own the farm next to the delightful Maureen here. Lovely to meet you, Reverend Ward. I must say you are much prettier than old Weeks, God bless him." Conrad walked across no-man's-land to vigorously shake my hand. "Maybe we should get a lady vicar in to replace you, Cattermole, old boy? Would make attending church a darn sight more attractive!"

Maureen slapped Conrad's thigh as he returned to his seat. "Conrad! Have more respect. I am sorry, Reverend," Straightening herself up she added, "And I am Maureen Sykes. As you all probably know, Judith, there, is my cousin."

"Lovely to meet you all."

The 'Walkers' now took turns to introduce ourselves before our collective eyes came to rest on the last members of our little group who had yet to speak. The two remaining 'Strollers' turned out to be a former army sergeant, now a physical education teacher, and the other a full-time mother and part-time Zumba instructor. The 'Strollers' were a fit bunch.

The rest of the meeting went well. We discussed some changes to the route from last year to add in a few more comfort break stops and the option of adding a shorter fun run for the children around Market Square for next year. I supported any suggestions that would remove the serious nature of an event that started life as a sponsored walk!

The second wave of plate filling and general chit-chat helped to clear both the air and the table of most of the remaining food as our visitors stocked up on extra jars of preserves before leaving. I bid goodbye to Reverend Cattermole, and we agreed to firm up any last-minute details over the phone.

"I've probably sold more today than Keith has at the market all morning!" laughed Judith as she and Maureen packed away the last couple of jars from the table. "Do you have any more rhubarb for me?"

"I left some with Keith before I came up. So kind of him to agree to watch my stall, too. He's such a sweetheart. You have a good one there, Cuz." Maureen winked at her cousin and offered a slightly crooked grin.

"Yup, he's a keeper!" Judith smirked in return. "Here, help me get this into the trailer and I'll give you a lift down the hill."

I watched the cousins giggling as they mounted Judith's quad bike. Further down the path, I caught sight of Helen Linden and Eunice Drinkwater chatting by the old oak tree. Most of the others were further down the road, edging their way closer to the cliff railway. It looked from where I stood that Conrad was calling back to the stragglers, urging them to catch up. It was hard to make out faces from this distance, though I could spot the 'Strollers' with their distinctive sweaters. Despite the rivalry, they behaved like an extended family planning their annual family reunion. I was looking forward to the 'Walkathon' now. It would be a fun day out and with Frederico's help, and the 'Otters' loss of Professor Linden, maybe it was finally time for Wesberrey to win.

Vengaboys

Tuesday evening brought the shared pain that is 'Walkers Workout'. I walked in late to find Frederico leading the rest of the 'Walkers' in a Latin American line dance. The Zumba beats of 'To Brazil!' by the Vengaboys gave everyone a catchy beat to try to stay in time to. Some were finding this harder to do than others, often with comical results. I quickly nipped into a space in the back row and whispered my apologies to the group. These easy steps were more difficult than they looked!

Frederico clapped his hands. "Okay. Let's take a short break. I hope you have all brought water with you. It is very important to drink water when you exercise."

I seized the opportunity to grab a few minutes with our instructor to apologise for the other night.

"No need to worry, Jess. Pão pão queijo queijo. Er, How you say? It is what it is."

Verity came over, her cerise lycra leotard barely holding her heaving bosom in place.

"Freddy, you sure know how to make a girl all hot and bothered."

It suddenly dawned on me that Verity was on her own. "Where's Avril tonight? She was so excited about the session at lunchtime."

"It's the weirdest thing, Vicar. We went back to the salon, and the team had everything in hand, so we both went home early to freshen up for the evening. Avril had ordered this gorgeous new tank top and..." Verity leaned in and covering her mouth with her hand in a melodramatic stage whisper added, "she wanted to, you know, de-fuzz. Anyway, as she was waiting for the wax to heat up, she grabbed herself some tea and toast. The next thing I know she was feeling a bit queasy and had locked herself in the bathroom. Probably had too much gluten today. She's a coeliac, but she loves bread and, well, I'm sure I saw her sneaking some of Barbara's cakes, too. She'll never learn. And the little piggy is supposed to be on a diet, she's lucky that top still fits her. Oink oink!"

"Oh, I am sorry to hear that. I hope she will feel better soon. I thought today's meeting with our rivals went very well. I hadn't realised how seriously they took everything. I wouldn't want to get on the wrong side of Miss Drinkwater."

"Oh yes, Eunice. Rumour has it she and Professor Linden had a massive row, and that's why she moved to the 'Strollers'. Being closer to work is just a smokescreen. Eunice can be... er, how can I put this? A little intense."

Frederico had slipped away during our conversation, and stationed back at the front of the hall, was limbering up for the next round of torture. He had amazing energy and re-silience. I could imagine that level of commitment in a relationship might be suffocating. The passion that attracted one to the other could soon become overwhelming. I wondered if that was what drove my sister to run away from the Brazilian god gyrating before me. I was really struggling to understand what else would make her leave him. Maybe, like Eunice, Frederico was just a little too intense. He certainly thought a lot of himself and his abilities, though he played down his more obvious charms. I suppose a man born that beautiful has never had to worry about being attractive. Maybe that was why he had chased Zuzu across the world? Maybe his mind could not reconcile itself with the reality that someone might not want him. His tanned face now looked extremely concerned.

"Jess! Slide to the left, the left!"

Barbara and I collided with such force we both now lay next to each other on the floor. Our legs so intertwined it was hard to tell whose trainers were whose. Frederico rushed over and offered me his hand, but I was laughing so much that I kept collapsing back down again. He tried to lift me from behind by pushing his arms through mine and dragging me up, but my feet couldn't find any traction with the floor. Despite Frederico's best efforts to pull me up, my giggling body kept defeating him. I imagine I resembled a new-born foal.

"Just leave me here," I choked. "I'll be alright in a moment."

Frederico stood tall and with an authoritative clap of his hands, dismissed the group for the evening.

Barbara had rolled herself onto all fours and crawled towards me. Struggling to catch her breath, she joked. "I think we need a nice cup of tea, Vicar. Too much exercise is bad for your health."

Barbara, Barbara, Wherefore Art Thou?

I awoke to find parts of my body aching that I really didn't know I even had. Frederico's workouts were extremely thorough, and he had tested all of our abilities last night. The collision with my parish secretary hadn't helped either, and I now had a sore rear end to add to my general aches and pain. I rolled over and sat on the side of my bed, my feet too tired to search out my cosy slippers. I hate to admit it, but I was exhausted. It felt like my future self had travelled back in time and pummelled me whilst I slept. All to show me how bad things would be on a daily basis if I didn't take better care of myself. A lesson I was in no mood to heed. Would my future self really mind if I just rolled back under the warmth and comfort of my snuggly duvet?

The ringing vicarage phone shattered my physically induced stillness. I cast a half-opened eye over to my alarm clock and noted the time. Six-thirty! The sun was just beginning to wake herself up. It was no time for any rational person to be calling another.

I forced myself out of the bed and crept towards the landing. My hunched future self was still in full possession of my broken-down body, according to the shadow it cast on the wall. The ancient answerphone downstairs picked up before I had even reached my bedroom door.

Bleep: "Vicar? So sorry. Barbara here. Oh, how I hate these things. Sorry, er, I must have caught a chill last night in that drafty hall. I'm not feeling too great. I spent most of last night on the bog! Too much information? Sorry. Anyway, I don't think I'll be able to work today. I hope to make the PCC tonight. Call me if you need anything." Bleep.

It was very unlike Barbara to take a day off sick, so I crawled down the stairs to call her back. She must be really unwell.

"Barbara? Jess here. Sorry I missed your call. It took me an age to climb out of bed this morning. Everything hurts after last night. How are you feeling?"

"Oh, don't you go worrying about me, Vicar. I just overdid it. Caught a chill, that's all. Phil is coming over later to, er…" I thought I could hear a muffled clearing of her throat. "He will check in on me."

I found their not-so-secret attraction amusing. Barbara's coyness was very endearing. They were both in their mid-fifties!

"Well, if you need anything, just let me know. And don't worry about this evening's meeting. You left some cake slices from yesterday in the vestry kitchen. We're well served for tasty goodies. So you rest, I will need you fighting fit to help me plan Easter week."

This is the life of an English vicar. I am always thinking ahead to the next festival or the next sermon. Lent is an interesting time. Forty days and nights that echo our Lord's time in the desert. It's a time of reflection. Time to strip away the trappings of the modern world and take some time to think about what is truly important. It is not just about giving up sweets so we can gorge ourselves on an abundance of overpriced chocolate eggs on Easter Sunday. It is a time to raise ourselves out of our winter hibernation and set out our intentions for the year ahead. What seeds are we planting? What will be our harvest?

I dragged my aching limbs into the kitchen. With a full house, it was rare to find this room empty these days. Today was one of those rare occasions. It was just me and Hugo, who weaved his fluffy black tail around my legs in the certain expectation of some tinned tuna.

The sun was stretching her rays through the white clouds. Maybe, my future self was right. I decided to join the sun in her morning practice. Standing in the small shaft of light that was streaming in through the glass in the back door, I lifted my tired arms to the heavens. I reached up as high as I could before releasing my torso down to touch the ground. I repeated this movement several times. Each time edging my body taller before I relaxed into the floor. It amazed me I could still touch my toes! The feeling of dangling was freeing. I straightened up slowly and stood in 'Wonder Woman' pose, legs apart, hands on hips and breathed in the morning air, the sun warming my face.

Maybe next time I could do this in the garden? I mused to myself as I turned to grab the kettle to make coffee. Do some yoga? Reconnect mind, body, and spirit.

"Listen to yourself, Jess. You sound like your mad aunt Cindy! You'll be casting rune stones and reading the tarot next." I muttered as I reached inside the fridge for some milk.

Alone at the table with a steaming cup of prime Columbian roast, I found my mind wandering to the family legend of fertility goddesses and keepers of wells. Aunt Cindy and I were childless. According to the family legend, that is no accident. The childless sister in a family of three daughters is destined to become the 'godmother'. I had become increasingly aware that things were different here on Wesberrey. I had strange experiences and sensations that I couldn't readily explain away. But I was a long way from accepting that I was next in line to inherit a truckload of pagan superpowers.

Being childless was not a blessing; it was not a curse, either. It was God's plan. His plan has always been for me to devote my life to spreading His love. I did not need children of my own to be a mother. I can provide a mother's love to my congregation. And I had parishioners to visit, so I had better get a move on and get to the bathroom before the rest of the house awoke.

Don't Panic, Don't Panic!

I was just about to leave on my daily rounds when the phone on the hall table rang again. This time I was close enough to pick up the receiver before it went to answerphone. It was from Sam.

"Jess, do you have a few minutes?" Sam's voice seemed agitated.

"Well, I was just on my way out but I can chat for a few minutes. What's up?"

"Are you aware of anyone from your 'Walkers' group feeling unwell?"

"Er, yes, Barbara rang in sick this morning, and Avril missed the session last night. Why?"

"I'm not sure just yet, but can you call them and tell them to come to the hospital straight away? Let me know if there are any problems getting them there. I can send transport. And can you and the other 'Walkers' come in too? Just for a few checks."

"Of course, but Sam, what's the matter? You sound very concerned. Should I be worried?"

"Jess, I'm sure it's nothing, but can you just get everyone in as soon as possible? Thanks. I need to go."

The main disadvantage of living on an island where cars are prohibited is that all other forms of transport are inherently slower. The advantage, of course, is that there are no traffic jams. In under an hour, all the 'Walkers' were at the Cottage Hospital being cared for by Martha and the rest of Sam's small nursing team in the hospital foyer. Rather worryingly, they were all wearing masks and surgical gloves. Barbara and Avril were whisked into small side wards as soon as they arrived.

Sam, as the hospital's clinical director, was too busy for me to interrogate, so I tried my luck with Martha.

"Reverend, it's not my place to tell yuh what's goin' on but Dr Sam had a call from Oysterhaven General first ting, and it seems a couple of 'Otters' were admitted there with similar symptoms. I heard Reverend Cattermole is very ill. Suspected kidney failure."

"Kidney failure!" I gasped, possibly too loudly if I wanted to maintain Martha's faith in my ability to keep a secret. I glanced across the foyer, relieved to see that no one appeared to have heard my cry. "Sorry, but kidney failure. That sounds very serious. I should contact the hospital and check on him."

Martha leaned in, obviously more wary now of being overheard. "Reverend, I heard he is in ICU."

I screwed up my forehead. "ICU? Oh, Intensive Care Unit. This is serious. And they think we might all have... whatever it is?"

"I tink Dr Sam just wants to be careful. I'm sure she'll tell yuh more later. Now, Reverend. I have work to do."

"Of course, of course. Thank you, Martha. God bless you."

I sat back down with the rest of the group. I couldn't understand how we could have the same malady as whatever had befallen the 'Otters'. We had only met them once. I needed to tell Sam that the whole group wasn't there at that meeting. Though both Barbara and Avril were. And Verity. If it's contagious, I suppose we could have spread it further at the workout session. I could be a carrier. My Mum? My sisters? Luke?

Suddenly, Phil rushed into the hospital, desperate to see Barbara. Martha, back at her usual station behind the reception desk, was trying to calm Phil down but was equally firm in telling him he had to wait elsewhere. Phil reluctantly took a seat at the far end of the room. I got up to go over to him and offer some comfort. But Martha scooted around from behind her desk and blocked me.

"Reverend, until we know what this is. I must ask yuh to stay away from Mr Vickers."

"But I am perfectly well, Martha. Well, except for a few aches and pains. Do you really think what they have is catching? If so, we need to tell my family and, oh my, what if I had missed Sam's call and gone out on my rounds already? I could have infected half the island! Maybe I already have!"

"Please, Reverend. Sit back down. As yuh said, yuh don't appear to have any symptoms. I'm sure Dr Sam will be with yuh shortly. Until then, we're just being careful."

I returned to my chair. Verity was understandably anxious about her sister and the fact that for the moment at least, she wasn't allowed to be with her. Judith was cuddling up to her husband, Keith. Her cousin Maureen was in Oysterhaven General, and they were waiting for news on her condition. Mandy and Audrey sat at either end of the main group, and Frederico was pacing back and forth like an army sergeant preparing for battle.

Unusually, no one was talking.

About an hour later, Sam emerged. Verity rushed over to my best friend, her clattering high heels echoing around the waiting area.

"Doc, any news on my sister? It's just her gluten-thingy, isn't it? I mean. Oh my! I was so mean. Blaming her for eating too much cake. She should have stuck to the salad! I snorted at her, Doc. Snorted. Little piggy sounds. I can't bear that being the last thing I said to her!"

"Miss Leybourne. Your sister is being cared for. I am confident all will be fine. We need to run a few more tests to confirm what is wrong, but she is strong. I can't say any more at the moment until all the results are in."

"Can I see her yet? No, silly, I'll sit back down. Or maybe not? She will need a new nightie. We didn't bring a bag. And her hair? Make-up? Doc, should I go home and…"

"I will let you know when you can go in. Please take a seat. I just want a quick word with Reverend Ward."

Sam ushered me into her office. Her 'professional' face dropped. Her brow furrowed. "Jess, I'm still waiting to get back some test results but I think Barbara and Avril were poisoned!"

"Poisoned? How? By who?"

"Who? You solve two murders and your mind automatically jumps to foul play!" Sam attempted a smile. "I am hoping it's accidental. But..."

"Do you think that's what is wrong with the 'Otters' too? Martha mentioned Reverend Cattermole is in intensive care."

"Yes, his kidneys are failing. But that is probably because of some underlying condition. I don't want to panic everyone."

Sam snapped off her cream surgical gloves and collapsed on her leather desk chair. It sprang back and forth from the shock. Sam allowed herself to rock along with it. When it came to a rest, she just sat there quietly with her head in her hands.

Her silence made me nervous. I admit, though, it was a relief to know I hadn't inadvertently been a carrier of some unknown virus. Looking at my best friend's weary face I wanted to help. "If it was food poisoning or something like that, at least it's not contagious."

Without lifting her head, Sam mumbled, "I guess that's something positive to hold on to."

I pulled the spare chair around to her side of the desk and sat down beside her. I took her hands away from her face to look into her worried eyes.

"I am sure you and your team will do whatever you can to help those affected. As you said, Avril is strong, and Barbara... well, nothing would dare try to kill off my parish secretary."

Sam sniffed. "Thank you. I had better put my face back on and go chase those results. It's just curious. They must have eaten the same thing?"

"Well, we all had cake at our meeting but, wait no we didn't. Barbara has given up sugar for Lent so she only had the savoury stuff and Avril is on a diet, though Verity claims she had a naughty nibble. A dodgy hummus, perhaps?"

"Hmm, perhaps. It's the timing I am struggling with. Avril was sick Tuesday evening. Barbara was fine. Her symptoms showed up later. I suppose there could have been a delayed response." Sam had taken off her tortoiseshell-rimmed glasses and was chewing the end of an arm as she mulled over the facts. Discovering the source of the poison presented her with an intriguing mystery, and she loved to solve a puzzle. It was quite the medical conundrum.

"Penny for your thoughts?" I was curious to know what was in her head.

"No deal, I'm sad to say. I had better get back to work. It would be a great help if you could just try to keep everyone calm."

"I will, of course. Perhaps we could say a little communal prayer?"

Sam sniggered. "Well, if that's your plan, wait till I am out of earshot first!"

"Heathen!" I joked back.

"Pragmatist."

"Sam Hawthorne, I've seen you in church."

"Yes, to support you! Anyway, this isn't the time." Sam stood and smoothed down her white coat. "You do your job. And I'll do mine."

***

Sam and her team were amazingly efficient at doing their jobs. They kept Barbara and Avril in for further tests and observations, but after a few routine checks, they allowed the rest of us to go home. No one else had any symptoms, though we were all advised to contact the hospital should we feel anything different.

I absentmindedly invited the group to return to the vicarage for a cup of tea, but everyone wisely declined. I suppose that was the best strategy until we found the source of the poison.

I was worried, though, about Reverend Cattermole and the other 'Otters'. It occurred to me that if something had poisoned them, then perhaps some of the 'Strollers' were ill, too. Reverend Cattermole would have contact information for everyone who attended the meeting yesterday and though he was in hospital, his secretary might be able to access those details for me. I was sure that St. Mildred's was one of the fading numbers taped to the hall desk next to the phone in the vicarage. I quickened my pace.

Familiar voices greeted me from the kitchen. I recognised them to be my sister Zuzu and her latest beau, Inspector Dave Lovington. My sister's flirtatious giggling warned me it was probably best not to burst in on them just yet so, once I had taken off my hat and coat, I went straight to call the vicarage in Oysterhaven.

"Hi, is that St. Mildred's? Reverend Jess Ward here from St. Bridget's. I was hoping to speak to the parish secretary."

"That would be me, Reverend. Lucky you caught me. I was just about to go up to visit Reverend Cattermole. How can I help you?"

"Oh, sorry, I won't keep you. I was just wondering if you have the phone numbers of all the people who came to visit Wesberrey yesterday. Just so I can check up on them. Find out how they are. Offer my support."

"Hmm, it's quite the list, Reverend, and I was on my way out. Can I post them to you?"

Post? That would take forever!

"I'm sorry. Look, I know it's a big ask. Could you maybe email them to me?"

"Oh, Reverend Ward, I don't hold with all that new fancy computer stuff. I will take the list with me to the hospital and post it to you from the post-box on the High Street. What time is it? Hmm... if I catch the twenty past bus I should make the last post before visiting hours."

I looked at my watch. *Or I could catch the next ferry.*

"Thank you, but don't bother posting the list. I will hop over and come to see Reverend Cattermole myself. Kill two birds with one stone, so to speak. Shall I meet you there?"

"As you wish, Reverend. I'll see you later."

I threw my coat back on, grabbed my helmet and jumped onto 'Cilla'. I had the strangest feeling that there was something afoot, and I needed to find out what was going on. A new adventure was about to begin.

Oysterhaven General

The Cottage Hospital on Wesberrey is a small Victorian red brick gothic style building that had adapted over the years to embrace modern medical practices. In contrast, the General at Oysterhaven, built in the late sixties, is modernity on a large scale. Set at the far end of the old High Street, it's usually only a fifteen-minute drive from the ferry port on the mainland side.

Oysterhaven also has a medium-sized shopping mall, a selection of secondary schools and other essentials of modern life like a leisure and sports centre. As a town, it is functional, *if not particularly pretty.* Most of the buildings are boxy mid-century designs and the road system is a baffling network of roundabouts. I almost always get lost, and today was no exception. I was anxious that Reverend Cattermole's secretary would have abandoned all hope of seeing me and already left by the time I arrived.

I shouldn't have worried. I pulled up at the motorcycle parking bay outside the hospital entrance and a frail old lady wearing a padded purple anorak, wide-legged navy slacks and sensible navy shoes was waiting there to meet me.

"Reverend Ward, I presume." A gloved hand reached inside the purple anorak and handed me a brown envelope. It all felt very covert.

I dismounted 'Cilla' and unclipped my helmet strap. "Yes, thank you. I'm sorry. I didn't ask your name."

"Prudence Beckworth. I believe you have already met my son Conrad?" Taking the envelope with a gracious smile, I nodded. "I hope he was behaving himself, Reverend. Conrad is a good boy really, but sometimes his humour can get him into a lot of trouble."

I found it quaint that Conrad, who must be firmly in the grip of middle-age, was being described as a 'good boy'. A mother's eyes, I suppose, though Conrad certainly had a playful nature.

"Thank you for the list. It really is very kind of you to wait for me here. I got a little lost with the roundabouts and one-way systems. Do we know how many of the 'Otters' are unwell?"

"Well, Conrad is fine. I heard that Eunice was feeling unwell, but she wasn't admitted to hospital. Only Richard and Maureen, so far. They were on the third floor. Seacole Ward. But then they took the poor reverend to the ICU. He is very sick, Reverend Ward; I am so worried about him." Tears sprang from Prudence's eyes. "I have worked for him for twenty years. He is such a kind man. So gentle. Never married." She shook her head. "He is like a son to me."

I put my arm around her quivering shoulders. "Well, I will do whatever I can to help, Mrs Beckworth. We will support each other through this, okay? My secretary is in hospital on Wesberrey. May I call upon your experience running a parish sometimes?"

"Of course, Reverend." Prudence produced a handkerchief from inside the sleeve cuff of her anorak. "Thank you." She sniffed. "You should get up to ICU pretty sharpish if you want to see Richard, sorry, Reverend Cattermole during visiting time. They are very strict. As it should be."

"Thank you. I will call you in the morning to discuss how we can keep both parishes going. Does that sound ok to you?"

She blew her nose, snuck the scrunched handkerchief back up her sleeve, and then produced a half-eaten tube of mints from her pocket. I wondered what else she secreted within the purple padding. "That sounds like a plan, Reverend." She offered me a mint.

I politely declined. "Well, have a safe journey back to Wesberrey. We will get through this together, eh?"

I felt that a hug should be offered and was pleased that it was accepted. Prudence was obviously anxious. After we said our goodbyes, I headed straight to the Intensive Care Unit.

***

I was not sure what to expect. I had visited many hospital wards and ICU departments in my work but I always find that initial entrance a disturbing experience. It is hard to see the person you are visiting lying on a hospital bed with various tubes and machines attached to them. There is a stillness that belies the frantic efforts to save lives that are taking place.

Reverend Cattermole was in the ward on the far left of the unit. The door to his room was closed, so I asked the station nurse if it was ok to go in. He looked at my dog collar (which is often a free entry pass) and advised me to wait in the family area. He would let me know when it was okay.

The twenty or so minutes I waited in the tiny room next to the service lift allowed me to quieten my mind and spend a little time talking to my Boss. I have often found these unscheduled opportunities for silent prayer to be very restorative, but today my mind wouldn't rest.

How could so many people fall ill so suddenly? If Sam was right, and it was poison, how was it administered? Was it a simple case of poor food hygiene or something more sinister? A random thought entered my head. Previously, I had had what some people would call a vision. I had seen shadows of the crime scene. I had felt their pain. If there was anything to this 'godmother' nonsense, then maybe I could connect consciously to that 'gift'. Channel it somehow. So, after apologising to the big guy for testing this pagan stuff out, I closed my eyes and tried to focus.

Nothing.

Perhaps I should try picturing the meeting yesterday?

Nothing.

Maybe if I focused on someone who was ill?

Nothing.

Okay, what about the food? If it was poison, surely the food was the most likely agent.

Nothing.

I felt exhausted.

This was stupid! I had no special 'gift'. I had been associating too closely with my mad aunt, and her special brand of crazy was rubbing off. That was all. This 'godmother' stuff was complete nonsense.

I smugly returned to my preferred state of prayer and contemplation. I have a working relationship with the one true God. He is the most benevolent boss. I didn't need all this other mumbo-jumbo.

***

My visit with Reverend Cattermole was extremely brief. The poor man was very ill. On various drips, a ventilator and a kidney dialysis machine, he could not communicate beyond a slight nod of the head and a blink of his eyes. I stayed by his bedside for a few minutes, and then the medical team appeared to do another set of tests. That was my cue to leave.

As I walked back through the winding hospital corridors, following the yellow line leading me back to the exit, I prayed in my heart for all those who were suffering. It was all I could do. Except, perhaps, to find the cause of the poisoning.

Time is Fleeting

Back on the Island, I still had some time before the weekly PCC meeting so I headed to the hospital to catch a few minutes with Barbara and reassure her we would be fine this evening without her.

My normally vibrant secretary looked as white as the hospital sheets she lay on. Her eyelids were heavy and her breathing laboured. "Thank you for coming, Reverend. I know you are extremely busy. The PCC starts in a few minutes, I'm so sorry to have let you down."

"Hush now, Barbara. Whilst we miss you terribly, we will struggle through without you. I'm perfectly capable of making everyone a cup of tea. You know, the men might even brew a pot themselves!"

"And the food? You know how Phil loves my cakes, and I was planning on bringing up some soup this evening. It gets so cold sitting around in the hall like that. That old heater barely warms itself up."

"Barbara, we will be fine. We still have some cake slices left from yesterday." The thought they could be the source of the poison re-entered my head. "Ah, yes, maybe we shouldn't eat them under the circumstances." I realised how foolish my words had been the moment they left my stupid mouth.

"Reverend, it can't have been my food. I am clean to the point of obsession!"

"I know. I didn't mean you did anything wrong. It can't have been the cakes. You have given up sugar for Lent. Maybe one of the dips had gone past its sell-by date or —"

"Reverend, it can't be my food. It can't be. I could never live with the knowledge I harmed all these souls with my incompetence!" Barbara was wringing the bedsheets in frustration.

"You are anything but incompetent! You are amazing. I don't know how you do it. It could be anything. Perhaps even that old heater you were talking about. Lord knows what fumes come out of its old elements."

***

The PCC meeting was functional but lacked its normal conviviality. Phil was particularly withdrawn. The concern for Barbara's health within the group was palpable.

At the close of business, Rosemary, church organist and long-standing PCC treasurer, accompanied me into the kitchen to help wash up the cups. "Is Barbara very ill?"

"I believe it could have been a lot worse if Dr Sam hadn't called us all in. At least she is being treated now. I think she'll be fine." I realised my words were not very reassuring. I placed my hand on Rosemary's arm. "She's a fighter. It'll take more than a few sour ingredients to do for Barbara."

"Poor Phil. He feels so helpless." Rosemary shook her bowed head as she placed a rinsed cup in the draining board to her side. "That man needs to fix everything."

"Rosemary, excuse me if this seems insensitive, but are Phil and Barbara... or have they ever been... in a relationship? They blatantly care for each other deeply, and there is such an obvious attraction."

"Ah, Reverend. Nothing gets past you. The tragic answer is no, and I have absolutely no idea why." Rosemary put down the final washed cup and dried her liver-spotted hands on the tea cloth. "Everyone else can see it, too. It's been like this for years. Phil bought the pub, what, the best part of fifteen years ago now, and Barbara has carried a torch for him from day one. She is old-fashioned and would never make the first move, so she just flirts and hopes he will take the bait. He flirts back but never bites. It is a well-worn dance." She sighed.

"Fifteen years of flirting!"

"Yes." I thought I saw Rosemary rolling her eyes in exasperation. "You youngsters don't realise how little time you have." Recalling my earlier conversation with Prudence, I smiled at being viewed as 'young' by anyone. Age is relative, though, and middle age is nothing to someone in their twilight years. In all things, the only time we are certain of is now. As to love, my sister was a testimony that it is never too late for a new romance. Rosemary sighed wistfully. "Maybe this brush with death will make him realise time is fleeting."

Phil had given Sam access to all the stored food from yesterday's meeting to take test samples earlier in the afternoon so, as we cleaned up, we moved the rest of the cakes and savouries to the food recycling bin. Like many of her generation, Rosemary was uncomfortable with such waste.

"We don't even know this food is dangerous." She tutted as she scraped the remains of a carrot cake into the small grey caddy next to the sink.

"Better to be safe than sorry." I tried to sound positive as I wiped down the worktop with a cloth soaked in disinfectant, but having just left Barbara's bedside, I was far from feeling hopeful.

The Baron

With Barbara still in the hospital, I woke up extra early to tackle head-on my growing list of tasks for the day. Though the house was calm, I was not alone. Hugo had curled himself up on a shelf above the radiator, and the brighter mornings had brought out the birds to keep me company with their uplifting chorus. I worked through steadily until my older sister interrupted my peaceful haven.

"Jessie, can I borrow 'Cilla' to go to the mainland?"

"Er, possibly. Where are you heading to?"

"To Stourchester. The 'Baron' is feeling a little under the weather. He never takes a day off work so, I thought if he's confined to his bed, he could do with some, er, company?" 'The Baron' has become Zuzu's pet name for Dave since she found out he is the fourth son of a baronet. It's not something she uses in front of him, though. I don't believe he would find it so endearing.

"What's wrong with him? Nothing serious, I hope."

"Nah, I think he has a cold or something. He just needs a little Zuzu magic." My sister grabbed the far corner of my desk and playfully shimmied up and down. She threw back her blonde mane and sighed. "We have been behaving for so long! The man is fit to burst!"

I wanted to say no. I'll be honest, I wasn't particularly enamoured with thoughts of Dave 'bursting' over my sister. I may be a vicar, but I'm not immune to the fallout of unrequited love.

"I'm not sure 'Cilla' will make it to Stourchester." I coughed. "Perhaps you should take the bus or train. Yes, the train from Oysterhaven would be quicker, especially if he is fit to bursting!"

"Hmm, maybe a train would be easier, then I needn't worry about getting 'Cilla' back to you." Zuzu perched crossed-legged on the corner of my desk tossing my scooter keys in the air and catching them with one hand. "You know, I might be home late, or I could get a one-way ticket? Just in case." She winked.

Boy, sometimes I hated and adored her in the same breath. "Yup, that sounds like a plan." Could my teeth be more gritted? "Off you go then, the ferry leaves in forty minutes."

"Thanks, Jessie. Er, I don't suppose you have any money, for the ticket?"

I pulled some notes from my purse and folded them into her waiting hand. "Just don't wear him out, okay? The mean streets of Stourchester need protecting."

"I won't. By the way, if you see Freddy tonight, wish him luck for his interview tomorrow. Love you!" And with an air kiss, she sashayed out the door.

Freddy? Tonight? I had completely forgotten about Thursday's instalment of 'Walkers' Workout. Though how many of us were still standing, I had no idea. Next on my To-Do list, phoning around all the 'Walkers', 'Strollers' and 'Otters' to check up on everyone. It would be a practical distraction from unwanted thoughts of my sister and 'The Baron'.

***

An afternoon of phone calls and emails helped me to put together a rough list of all the potential victims of the mysterious poison.

From the 'Walkers' it had affected only Avril and Barbara. In Oysterhaven, Maureen and Reverend Cattermole were in hospital, but no one else appeared to be unwell. Eunice confirmed over the phone that though she had felt *slightly* under the weather, she didn't feel the need to go to the hospital. I urged her to get checked out by her local doctor at the very least, which she promised she would do. All the other 'Otters' seemed unharmed.

The 'Strollers' proved more difficult to contact. I eventually spoke to Sonia via email, engaging in a lengthy back-and-forth that would have been much quicker if conducted over the phone. The upshot of the conversation was that she was well and would see Professor Linden for a tutorial the following morning. Sonia told me she hadn't heard of any 'Strollers' falling ill but would send a WhatsApp message to their group and let me know if the situation changed. I mentioned I was visiting the university with Frederico the following day, and it would be a lovely idea to meet for lunch. Sonia offered to invite the professor to join us.

My last call of the day was to Prudence to work out the timings for Sunday Service so we could take advantage of the change to British Summer Time, enabling me to conduct both masses with minimal disruption to parishioners' lives. I could run my regular service at the advertised time (thanks to the clocks going forward an hour) and by pushing back the service at St. Mildred's, I would face a happy congregation there who had the gift of an extra hour in bed.

A Day Trip to Stourchester

F riday brought with it heavy rains and howling winds. The weather report on the radio confirmed that a storm with a female name was whipping itself into a frenzy across the Irish coast, and the trail winds were stretching almost as far south as the Channel Islands. Any ferry crossings this morning were looking doubtful. Zuzu had phoned home last night to tell us she was staying with 'The Baron' and given the weather, it was unlikely she would return home today. This news caused much tutting and eye-rolling from my mother.

My predominant concern was getting Frederico to his interview safely and on time. I had agreed to travel with him to keep him company. Frederico approached all activities with military precision, and I didn't doubt for a moment that he had prepared for the journey ahead. He had travelled halfway across the world to find my sister, so I was sure he could navigate his way through the cobbled streets of Stourchester. But he was still in a foreign land, alone, and I felt that it was the very least I could do to support him.

If the ferries were running, Bob McGuire would already be down at the ferry port and unreachable by phone, so I thought I would call his sister Mandy. She might give me an update on the crossing situation.

"Mandy? Reverend Ward here. Frederico and I need to get to Stourchester, and I was wondering if you had any news on the ferries?"

"Good morning, Vicar. I'm afraid I don't. No. Erm, if the seas are becoming too choppy for ships, the lighthouse usually sounds the foghorn. So I think you're okay to leave if you get there quick enough. Coming back might be an issue as the storm moves closer. I suggest you both have a back-up plan. Just in case."

"Mandy, that is a very sensible suggestion, thank you." Talking aloud to myself, I added. "Maybe we could stay at St. Mildred's vicarage?"

"That sounds like a marvellous idea, Vicar. I have to dash. Need to get the kids to school. See you tomorrow. Bye!"

Mandy put down the phone before I could answer. Her urgency was something I needed to adopt if we stood any chance of getting to the mainland. I called Phil at the 'Cat and Fiddle' to alert Frederico and tell him I would meet him at the ferry port in thirty minutes.

We were both there in twenty.

Just in time, it transpired, to catch the last ferry out. Safely deposited on the mainland, with time to spare before the next train to Stourchester, we treated ourselves to breakfast at the 'Whistlestop' cafe next to Oysterhaven railway station. The distant foghorn called Bob back to the island as the storm rolled in.

Frederico opted for a healthy, carb-free avocado and egg salad. My choice was carb-free too, if you took out the buttered toast, and really healthy if you removed the fried eggs, bacon, and hash browns. *The grilled tomatoes and mushrooms were good choices, right?* My shame lessened slightly by us both ordering extra large coffee lattes, though Frederico's was with coconut milk and didn't have a double shot of caramel syrup.

The 'Whistlestop' cafe was a quirky railway-themed eatery which tripled up as an artisan bakery and a local art gallery. Its eclectic style worked. The dated black stack music system from the Eighties played an intriguing tape of pre-war jazz and popular swing tunes. The mix of Bing Crosby and crispy bacon was rather delightful.

"Are you nervous about the interview?"

"Não estou preocupado. I am not worried." he shrugged. "Minha amiga, do not concern yourself about me. I am a man who thinks clearly about such things."

"Frederico, you are an intelligent man. I don't know why she left you, but I can tell you that there is no point in waiting around. My sister never looks back."

"You have said this. Zuzu has said this. But I never lose."

His face darkened with a serious intensity. He was a man on a mission, and the next part of his strategy was to secure this job. I found myself torn between wishing him well and suppressing a growing concern about where this would all end.

The wind outside the cafe rattled the street signs. Its erratic behaviour mirrored my own unsettled mood. Frederico's attitude was probably just male bravado, I told myself. No need for alarm. He travelled across the globe to win my sister back. It is natural to want to do everything he could to achieve that goal. Surely, once he understood it was a lost cause, he would move on, emotionally if not physically.

***

Rain raced down the carriage window in little streams that swelled into a mini river at the bottom of the pane. Condensation from the heat of the carriage hitting the biting cold outside clouded my view of the countryside we sped past, but I still preferred to look at that than to continue to face my stern travelling companion. As we drew ever closer to Stourchester, Frederico's mental focus on his battle plan intensified. There was no room for small talk and no space for anything pertaining to my sister not being his ultimate prize.

We walked in silence from the station to the university and arrived with a good half hour's grace before his interview slot. I had a date with my niece's boyfriend, Dominic, which now gave me the perfect excuse to bid Frederico good luck and make a quick exit. As our exact timings for the day were still a little vague, Frederico and I agreed to text each other later. *What did we do before mobile phones?*

I cannot express the relief I felt walking away.

***

In contrast, my soul danced at the sight of Dominic's floppy hair and broad smile. It was easy to see what Freya saw in him. They had fallen head over heels the moment they met, back on that chilly January day, in Market Square. In fact, if there was ever an argument for love at first sight, I think they were it. I contemplated what beautiful babies they could create.

That's if Freya isn't the next 'godmother'. I shook my head to clear away that unwanted thought. This stupid family myth! It was a freaky generational coincidence and nothing more. What deity could deny this gorgeous couple their own children, if that's what they planned?

Back when we first met on Wesberrey, Dominic had greeted each lady present with a gallant kiss on the hand. So, I held my right hand out in anticipation. The poor boy looked uneasily around the quad.

"Er, sorry, Reverend Ward, but that would look a bit weird here. Happy to give you a hug, though."

"A hug would do just fine." I laughed. "It's such a tonic to see you again. How have your studies been going?"

"Ah, yes. Very well. I have my final assessment just after the Easter break and then the end-of-year show. Do you want to see what I'm working on?"

I nodded. Knowing this young man's love of the Pre-Raphaelites I hoped in my heart, that whatever his project, it would be both beautiful and full of pathos.

Dominic ushered me through the gothic corridors to a yard at the rear and a large corrugated metal hangar where the art students worked. Not having a single artistic bone in my body I am always in awe of the process. All around the workshop were pieces in various stages of development. The smell of paint and turpentine was literally breath-taking. It was impossible not to react to the heady mix of industry and beauty.

At the far corner stood a large wooden easel supporting an even larger canvas covered in a grey tarpaulin sheet speckled in paint.

"I hope you like it."

A nervous Dominic pulled back the cover to reveal a portrait dominated by two corn-flower eyes, literally cornflowers as eyes, set upon a milky complexion dotted with gold freckles. Her lips were actual rose petals and her hair, copper coils, which both cascaded down and danced across the canvas. It was magnificent and clearly inspired by my niece. Though abstract, it caught her vitality. It felt alive.

"Wow!"

I had wanted to respond with an intelligent remark that would demonstrate my deep appreciation of art, but I don't really have any real understanding beyond knowing if I like it or not. 'Wow' may not have been an intellectual response, but it was genuine.

"So you like it, then? It's inspired by Freya.' I mused that his muse was never in doubt.

"I have called it 'A Goddess for the Millennium'."

"Well, I am sure it will delight her. She's coming back for the Easter break. I know she can't wait to see you."

His rosy cheeks vanished as his entire face blushed to a sweet shade of strawberry pink. He really was adorable. *Young love, so carefree and hopeful.*

"I've missed her so much, Reverend Ward." He flipped his hair back and casually threw himself down on a battered old sofa. The workshop was full of random objects and odd items of furniture. "I am counting the days and nights. I have never felt like this before. I doubt anyone has in the history of mankind. No love song or poem comes close to how I feel. I can paint nothing else. Her and only her."

"Well, you have captured my niece's spirit perfectly."

***

We talked more over a coffee in the refectory where Sonia joined us at just after one o'clock, as agreed.

"Sonia, hope you are hungry. My treat. Dominic tells me they do an amazing fish and chips here on a Friday. The chips come in a tiny metal bucket on the side, very chic. Not at all like my university days. What would you both like?"

I left the two students to introduce themselves whilst I joined the food queue. Even the university has a more contemporary food choice than we have on Wesberrey. The only choice on the island is the pub or a fancy French restaurant with prices that only the fourth son of a baronet could afford. My sister could definitely pick them, I thought as I stood in line. I wondered how the interview was going. I understood from Frederico it was quite a lengthy process that involved a presentation, panel interview, and an academic *viva voce*. At least I was spending my downtime in pleasant company. The rain outside was not letting up. If anything, it seemed to be getting worse.

The refectory had momentarily run out of fish, so they took my money and promised a server would bring it over as soon as it was ready. I returned to find Dominic and Sonia fast friends.

"You didn't tell me that Sonia is studying feminist history."

I lay down settings of knives, forks and paper serviettes I had collected at the till. "Well, I don't think Sonia actually told me. Is that what Professor Linden lectures in?"

"Yes, she is a world-renowned authority on women and the Enlightenment, especially Mary Wollstonecraft. She is also passionate about pagan matriarchal societies. She is very keen to talk to you, Reverend Ward, about the established church and the oppression of women."

"Well, historically I might agree with her, though I think the Church is making huge strides to address that. Did you invite her to join us for lunch? How was your tutorial?"

As I spoke the waiter came over with our food. It smelt delicious. Three large plates of golden cod fillets with chunky fat chips and side orders of mushy green peas. A traditional English gift from the gods. The three of us fell silent as we each dived into our offerings of crispy batter and snow-white fish steaks. That first mouthful was simply divine.

Sonia interrupted our gastronomic rapture to answer my earlier question.

"She never showed. I waited outside her office for half an hour, nothing. I guess she got held up somewhere. The problem is there's nowhere to sit. It's a very narrow corridor. So I had to go. People kept tripping over me. I sent her a text telling her to join us, though. This is great fish. Chips are a little soggy. But thanks, Vicar. Much appreciated."

Sonia gobbled up the rest of her plate and didn't say another word. Once finished, she apologised that she had a lecture to get to. Mumbled something about looking forward to the 'Walkathon' in two weeks. Then she left.

Dominic and I looked at each other and burst out laughing.

"She's quite a character!" Dominic returned to his meal. "Feminist history must really make you hungry!"

"Well, it looks like Fine Art does too," I said, pointing to his almost empty plate. "Fancy joining me for some dessert? I noticed they had some type of crumble. Just what the doctor ordered on a day like this." The sky outside was now so dark with rain the sun had taken the rest of the day off. "I don't think the ferry will run this evening." Opening my purse, I pulled out a ten pound note and slid it across the table. "I think I need to call St. Mildred's. When you're ready, get me some dessert."

Dominic dutifully cleared his plate and went up for 'afters'. I turned on my mobile to call Prudence. There was a text from Frederico. His interview was due to end at 4 pm. Excellent. Plenty of time to relax and have a lovely cup of tea.

Love is War

After a pleasurable, if blustery, afternoon touring the historic grounds of Stourchester University with my enthusiastic guide, I settled myself down with a book in the main reception to wait for Frederico. I really hoped that his mood would be better after the interview. If the weather forced us to take shelter at St. Mildred's, I wanted to spend a pleasant evening together without this morning's intensity.

Around four o'clock I received a text message. But not from Frederico.

"Jessie, it's the Baron. Can you come to Stourchester A & E?"

Frederico was due out any minute. What was I supposed to do? I had to call my sister.

"Zuzu? What's up? What's happened?"

"It's Dave. I am in the ambulance with him now." My sister's speech was clearly agitated. "Can you come to the hospital? You are still in Stourchester, right?"

"Yes, I am, but…" What was I supposed to do with her ex-lover? Take him with me? Send him alone to St. Mildred's?

A quick glance out the reception window confirmed that the weather was not letting up. The clouds above grew dark and heavy. The branches of the courtyard trees were bending wildly in response to the raging wind. The sea would be too much for a small ferryboat. We were certainly staying here for the night.

"I will have to bring Frederico with me. I'm not sure how that will work. How bad is he?"

"Jessie, he's in a bloody ambulance! It's bad!" My sister was near hysterical. I could feel her frustration and panic clawing at me through the airwaves. "Jessie, I need you. Please. I can't lose him. I love him. I don't think I have ever really loved anyone before. Not like this. I can't do this!"

She loves him.

Tears swelled my eyes.

I took a deep breath and pushed my selfish thoughts back where they belonged.

"Zuzu, try to stay calm. Dave's strong. There's lots of life left in him. Why did you call the ambulance?"

"His breathing. Jess, we were... er, we had been having a splendid time. He was unwell but still, I mean. He's strong, you're right. Magnificent, in fact. But then he couldn't breathe! I thought he was having a heart attack!"

There was a beeping sound on my phone. It was probably Frederico trying to contact me.

"Sis, I will get there. Okay? I need to deal with Frederico first. Love you. Alright? He will be fine, I promise."

I switched calls. It was indeed Frederico. He said he was nearly there. He could see me through the glass. What was I going to do? I walked slowly to the doorway, buying my brain as much time as possible to think of a plan. "Ah, Frederico! How did it go?"

"As expected. The job is mine. Tenho certeza. I am certain."

"That's great!" Maybe I said that a little too eagerly. "Listen, Frederico. I just had Zuzu on the phone. She needs me. She is on her way to the hospital."

"The hospital? Minha namorada está doente? I must go to her!"

"No, she's fine. It is... it's not her... She is with someone."

"O Barão?" His mood changed. I thought I could detect a hint of schadenfreude. "I hope it is very serious."

"Frederico!" His candour shocked me.

"You want me to wish my enemy well?"

"Well, yes. It is the Christian thing to do."

"Amor é guerra. Love is, what is the word I need? War! Yes, love is war."

"Frederico, she needs me. She's my sister, and I have to go. Will you be able to find St. Mildred's? I'll call ahead and let them know you'll be arriving before me. You cannot take the ferry back tonight."

Of course he could find it. He found my sister with just a few clues on a postcard from thousands of miles away.

Cotton Sheets and a Jacuzzi

I caught up with Zuzu in the relatives waiting area in the Accident and Emergency Department of Stourchester Hospital. Three hospitals in as many days. This was becoming an unwelcome habit.

Hospitals all smell and sound the same. Once seated inside, it was easy to forget which one this was. The original 'Stourchester Infirmary' is built on the site of a seventeenth-century workhouse and is a dizzying maze of long, low-ceilinged corridors with small dingy wards branching off. There was little natural light. The A&E department, added after the Second World War, is a stark contrast to the Victorian main building, full of fluorescent bright light and colourful abstract art on the walls.

"So what happened? He had a cold, right?"

"Well, he just said he had a bit of a bug. He was already feeling better by the time I got there. In fact, he was full of energy. I teased him it was just a ruse to get me alone." For a moment, the misty recollection of a passion-filled evening replaced the stress on her face. "About eleven this morning, we had a late breakfast, you know, to keep us going." I really didn't want to think about what they needed to keep going. "Then we were on his sofa and he started having a panic attack or something. He couldn't breathe. I was so scared, Jessie."

"Have the doctors said anything?"

"They just took him straight in. As soon as I said he was Inspector Lovington, they just whisked him away. A nurse said she would come and get me later." Zuzu had been crying. Her blue eyes were pink and puffy. I rarely saw her rattled like this.

"C'mon, Sis. He'll be fine. Look, I'll see if I can find anything out. This collar makes people talk."

Seriously, I had no need for my aunt's fairy magic. People see my dog collar, and doors just open. Within seconds, I was standing in a curtained cubicle with the attending medical staff. The 'Baron' lay on the bed before me. An oxygen mask covered his mouth and nose. The mask's elastic ties pressed his hair to his head, and sweaty locks clung to his face. The green plastic mouthpiece reflected colour on his uncharacteristically pallid complexion. Despite Dave's smile as I approached, his eyes betrayed his fear.

A petite female doctor sporting a high ponytail of unbelievably glossy black hair was writing up her notes on a clipboard. "So, Dave," she said, clicking her pen and putting it back into her coat pocket. "Your vitals seem fine. A nurse will be along shortly to take some bloods, and we'll keep that mask on you for a little while longer. But you'll be fine. Just rest. Do what you are told and we will get you home as soon as possible. Okay?"

As she turned to go, I took my chance to get more information.

"Excuse me, Doctor. I'm Reverend Ward. The Inspector is my friend. I was wondering if you have any idea what has caused this?"

"We are running tests. His symptoms, though, suggest poisoning of some nature. The sudden onslaught, no previous ill health. Most likely from a dodgy kebab, knowing the police. They are always picking up poorly cooked food on shifts. His breathing is a concern but I will know more when we get the results back. Now, if you could excuse me I have to get to the next patient. We are very busy today."

"Thank you. Can he have visitors?"

"Oh, yes, he's not contagious. Of that, I'm sure." She looked at her watch and tutted slightly. "I doubt we'll get a bed for him before nine. As long as you keep noise to a minimum, he can have a maximum of two visitors at a time."

I nodded and thanked her, but I don't think she heard me. I went back out into the waiting room and brought my sister back in past the triage nurse on duty at the door.

All the nursing staff had left by the time we got back to the bed. Zuzu dragged across a neon-green plastic chair from the corner of the bay and sat on Dave's left side. I stood at the foot of the bed. Dave appeared to be fast asleep. Zuzu manoeuvred herself closer so she could comfortably take his hand through the side bed guard.

"Are you sure he will be ok? How could he have been poisoned? We only had toast."

"Did you have anything on the toast?"

"Just some of that jam you had. Dave really loved it when he was over the other day, so I thought I would bring it with me. You don't think it was that, do you?" The realisation that she might have unwittingly poisoned the 'love of her life' floored my sister. The stress of the situation was too much for her to bear. "I can't do this, Jessie! What if I had killed him? I couldn't go on. I don't like these feelings. It *hurts*!"

"You really love him, don't you?" I could see that this scenario was not what my sister was used to. My thoughts went to Frederico, probably making himself comfortable in Reverend Cattermole's sitting room at this very moment, plotting his next steps to win back her heart.

"Zuzu, I think they will keep Dave in overnight at least. Frederico and I are staying at St. Mildred's. There won't be any ferries because of the weather. You can join us. I am sure Reverend Cattermole won't mind, especially given the situation."

"I think I will go back to Dave's. I have his key."

"I get you don't want to stay overnight with Frederico but —"

"Jessie, I'm not worried about him! Believe me. I'm being totally selfish. The 'Baron' has Egyptian cotton sheets and a jacuzzi!"

I suspected uncovering that the ailing 'Baron' on the bed before us was part of the British aristocracy with a generous trust fund had made him very attractive. Who wouldn't fall for a dashingly handsome hero of means? But this time I think my sister's feelings genuinely ran deeper. My sister was finally in love.

I once thought he was very cute, too. Now, as I gazed down on this 'magnificent' man floored by whatever this poison was, I worried about him as a friend and a brother. Unlike Frederico, I understood the futility of my trying to change the situation and had moved on. Well, that was what I kept telling myself.

I stayed with my sister until the porters came to move Dave onto the ward. His breathing was better by then, and we had even exchanged a few words. I resisted talking to him about the poison. The source was obviously the jam. That was the only link between the people affected, and Dave felt worse after eating it again. I know Barbara said she had vowed herself off sugar for Lent, but my guess was that she had given in to temptation. She probably allowed herself a naughty midnight snack. The delay in exhibiting any symptoms supported that theory.

I was sure it was just the result of an error in the bottling process or something like that. I needed to talk to Sam as soon as possible. Poor Judith, news of this mistake could ruin her small business, and her cousin Maureen was still in the hospital.

I had quite a few calls to make.

***

After telling the doctors on the ward my suspicions about the jam, I urgently rang Sam on my mobile and then planned with Phil for him to go to Barbara's cottage to collect any remaining jars and take them to the Cottage Hospital for testing.

I still needed to phone Judith. I knew that this would be horrible news for her to hear.

But by now I was on the train.

Time to breathe.

The call to Judith could wait a few minutes.

I needed to speak to the big guy.

The clickety-clack and swaying of the train back to Oysterhaven provided the perfect metronome. Soon, with my breathing controlled and my focus centred, I tried to picture Judith in my mind. If I could see her, I could walk through how I would approach the conversation and, with the help of Our Lord, find the right words to impart the news whilst providing a balm for her anxiety. I was making myself open to being, as St. Francis of Assisi actually didn't say, a channel of his peace.

One thing St. Francis did write though was the 'Canticle of the Creatures'. What could I remember?

Praised be you, my Lord, through Sister Moon and the stars:

in heaven you formed them clear and precious and beautiful.

Praised be you, my Lord, through Brother Wind;

and through the air, cloudy and serene, and every kind of weather,

through which you give sustenance to your creatures.

Praised be you, my Lord, through Sister Water,

who is very useful and humble and precious and chaste.

Praised be you, my Lord, through Brother Fire,

through whom you light the night:

and he is beautiful and playful and robust and strong.

If I were to share those verses with my pagan family, they would say I was calling on the forces of nature. I see it as realising the power of God's creation.

I tried again to focus on Judith. Usually, I am good at seeing faces in my mind's eye, but that evening I was struggling. Every time I saw Judith, I would see Maureen. They are very alike, it's true. But then I would see Judith's husband, Keith. Then Eunice! Finally, my mind rested on to Professor Linden. Lord! At this rate, I would have conjured the faces of everyone entering the Wesberrey Walkathon! Obviously, my mind was too preoccupied. I admitted defeat, thanked my Boss for his time and eternal love, and searched for Judith's number on my phone. I would have to trust my own judgement.

A Cosy Night In.

I was soaked to the skin by the time I had walked from the station to St. Mildred's vicarage, and desperately hungry.

There is a familiar feel to most English vicarages that always give me a cosy vibe. The colours on the walls are usually warming shades of a particular green and country cream, though I have been in several that appeared to prefer the peculiar charms of mud brown. It's as if the Church of England received a job lot of paint back in the 1800s and everyone is still using up the reserves. Oriental rugs, that once reflected the privileged status of their residents, now lie tattered and threadbare upon polished wooden floors, unless they covered the boards with a hideous orange, swirly carpet from the sixties. Fortunately, there is never any shag pile, far too decadent for a vicarage. And to finish the look, scenes of country life and the portraits of previous tenants adorn the walls. This uniformity provides visitors with an instant connection to the clerics of times gone past and offers comfort to a modern soul.

From the same vicarage reserves spring forth parish secretaries and housekeepers. Prudence is traditional in look and temperament. Barbara, though more vibrant than most in her fashion sense and personality, equally embodies the calm and caring efficiency that provides a vital, if usually taken for granted, support. Therefore, as I expected, St. Mildred's secretary was ready to greet me at the door armed with a towel to dry my hair, sheets of newspaper on the floor of the hallway to absorb any drips, and a much-welcomed change of clothing.

"Reverend, I have made up a bed for you. Up the stairs, second door on your right. The bathroom is across the landing. I have seen to Mr D'Souza, who is relaxing by the fire in the lounge. But first, let's get you dry and fed. I will warm your dinner through. I hope you like chicken, fresh from the farm. Conrad brought it up earlier, bless him. I've made a nice casserole with dumplings."

"Thank you, Mrs Beckworth. You are too kind."

It had been several months, if not years, since my designated room for the night had received visitors. Though the bed linen was fresh today, and Prudence had attempted to air and dust the room before my arrival, it still had a musty scent. A distinct note of camphor permeated the heavy pink eiderdown and matching candlewick bedspread that weighed down the checkered bed sheets. As a person used to the freedom of a duvet, this would be a novel experience.

Not used to catering for female vicars, Prudence had provided me with a change of men's striped blue pyjamas and a rather fetching silk paisley housecoat. I was grateful now for Reverend Cattermole's hefty frame. The shirt comfortably sat over my bosom without the buttons pulling, and there was ample material in the gown to cover my modesty too.

The warmed casserole was delicious. Perhaps, as Mum suggested, I should get a house-keeper, especially if this is what I could look forward to coming home to after a long day of parish duties. At the moment, my house was full of people who cook. My mother loves to feed us and Rosie too is very domesticated, but I couldn't rely on them to keep feeding me. There was no way they would live with me long term. We had all led very independent lives, and I was sure even if we all stayed on the island, it wouldn't be long before everyone needed their own space.

"If it's okay with you, Reverend Ward, I will head off now. What time would you like breakfast in the morning?" I suddenly felt very selfish for keeping this elderly lady up so late. The fact that she might have to get home in this weather at this hour had not occurred to me.

"I'm so terribly sorry, how inconsiderate of me. Surely you are not venturing out tonight?"

"No, Reverend." Prudence laughed. "I have the room next to yours. I have lived here for nearly thirty years. The vicar at the time, dear sweet Reverend Manning, took me and Conrad in when we had nowhere to go. Conrad's father was a very violent man. I used to live on the farm but... I had no choice, you see."

"Ah, and Conrad inherited the farm when his father died?"

"Yes, once Conrad was a grown man and able to stand up for himself, he went back. A vicarage is no place for a young man. But I stayed on as housekeeper and secretary for Reverend Manning and then to Reverend Cattermole. Two kinder men you will never find. I keep him in my prayers, you know, Reverend. He's still in intensive care. But they say they are hopeful, the doctors. They're hopeful. That is good, isn't it?"

"Yes, it is good." I could see that Prudence was close to crying. Her love for Reverend Cattermole and her fear, not only for his health but obviously for her own future, was clear. "We could pray together if that will help?"

Prudence smiled her agreement and sat down at the table next to me. Hands joined, eyes shut, we prayed for the speedy recovery of all of our friends from this mysterious poison, with a special mention of Reverend Richard Cattermole at whose table we sat this evening. I felt strongly that the good Lord was listening. Tomorrow there would be better news.

***

I found Frederico sitting close to the crackling fire, enjoying a glass of Richard's scotch whiskey. He, too, sported a paisley silk gown, though I will admit it hung better from his broad shoulders.

"Minha amiga, I am sorry I did not join you. I have many thoughts." Frederico swirled the contents of his glass attentively. "This is a very fine single malt."

I knew his thoughts would be about my sister, and I wasn't in the mood to excuse or explain her behaviour or her decisions. It was not my business to say anything. Any conversations on that matter should be between them. However, I thought I should try to engage in some conversation. Ask about the interview. Make small talk.

I sat in the other armchair flanking the fireplace. The warmth of the hearth was inviting. It was easy to forget the howling storm that raged outside.

"That's okay, I was so hungry, I wouldn't have been very up for conversation anyway. How did your interview go?"

Frederico continued to concentrate on his drink. "I was impressive. It is fate, no? That a role in my field should be open now. Does it not suggest that it is right that I am here? That my cause is true?"

I shifted awkwardly in my chair. If I had doubted it before, this afternoon's display of love confirmed my view that Frederico's was a lost cause. "Maybe God's plan is for you to have a fresh adventure in England? Perhaps there is someone more wonderful waiting for you to see them across the university's venerable quads?"

"Hmm, it is a beautiful building, though its animal science department is archaic. There are more stuffed heads there than in the Museu de Zoologia da Universidade de São Paulo!" Frederico chortled and slapped his left thigh with his free hand.

I was probably sporting the enigmatic smile of an inferior intellect. Or at the very least, someone who couldn't speak Portuguese. My face half pretending to get the joke and half admitting I did not understand what he had just referred to.

Frederico shook his head. With pity in his voice for my limited knowledge, he added, "It is a museum in São Paulo with millions of preserved specimens of animal and insect life. The mammal collection alone has over 50,000 examples of the most exquisite taxidermied animals."

"Ah, I see, like the Natural History Museum in London. Very funny. Stuffed heads. I get it."

"I spent many years there as a boy, it is what made me want to study mammals. We are mammals too, you know. Just beasts, like any other. Our drives are as primal, we just pretend to seek a higher path. We all want to fulfil our most base desires. Is that not what religion is for? To... how do you say? Make believe that we are above all of that. But we are all just animals seeking to survive. We are the hunters and the hunted. Masters and prey. There is no right or wrong. There is just winning or losing. The winner lives to fight another day - and then we die."

"I believe there is more to the human experience than just survival. There is a bigger plan."

Frederico sat forward in his chair and turned to face me squarely as if preparing for battle. A battle of thoughts and words, a battle of wits and ideology. A battle I was way too tired to engage in.

"A bigger plan? Whose plan? His?" Frederico pointed above his head. "Tell me, do you believe *He* made the world in seven days? Hm?"

"Frederico, it is late, and I am tired. Perhaps we can revisit this theological debate another time?"

"But Jess, please answer me. Was that His plan? And was it His plan to punish all creatures because two people ate from the apple tree? To bring death and destruction to His perfect world like, what's that cartoon? You know, where the blue alien builds the cardboard city only to knock it all down and rip it apart with his teeth?"

"Lilo and Stitch?" I will admit, I didn't see that coming.

"Yes, Lilo e Stitch. Stitch is the monster, right? He is bad. But your God, he creates and destroys for fun, and yet he is good? If there is a God, minha amiga, he understands our passions and desires. He gave them to us to build on his creation, to explore. There is no stepping back. There is no giving up. You find what you want, what you need, and you fight for it."

There was a sinister glint in Frederico's eye. It could have been the reflection of the fire, but it made me shudder. I would have wondered if *Dave's* poisoning had a more malevolent source, if I didn't already know that it was the accidental ingestion of a dodgy batch of Judith's jam that caused it.

"It is an interesting debate, but I really need to sleep. Mrs Beckworth will expect us for breakfast at eight. Pleasant dreams."

Safely in bed, I shivered beneath my heavy eiderdown. I now understood why Zuzu had left Brazil. The charming, handsome, intelligent man downstairs is a psychopath.

Breakfast at St. Mildred's

B reakfast was the traditional British fare. By that I mean, everything that could be fried was fried. Frederico, ever mindful of his regime, arrogantly declined everything after the first course of porridge. Regardless, Prudence happily fussed around her guest, keen to get him to eat more. When she produced a pot of Judith's rhubarb jam, it was very tempting to join in with her earnest petitions. *For a moment. Just for a moment.*

"Prudence! Not the jam! We think that is the source of the poisonings."

"Oh, Reverend, I'm so sorry. I wasn't thinking, I mean. Oh my! So sorry. I'll make another pot of tea." She scuttled over to the kettle, which she then refilled noisily at the Belfast sink. The excess noise was meant to drown out her sobs. I laid down my knife and fork and went to give her a hug.

"Prudence, he will be okay. We will call the hospital together in a minute. As to the jam, you weren't to know. I'm curious, though, does Richard always have rhubarb?"

"No, not usually. When he brought it back, I was quite surprised. He is very much a creature of habit. Usually returns with a couple of jars of 'Hudson's Homemade Bakewell Tart' jam. He was very disappointed there were none at the meeting. Still, he thought he would try something new. And now he is..." The whistle of the boiling kettle drowned out her voice.

"Bakewell tart jam? I don't remember seeing that. Sounds interesting."

"It's just cherry and almond jam with a dash of vanilla essence. I said I would make him some myself. Perhaps I could do that, for when he comes home? I could get the ingredients from the supermarket. They have everything I need there, marvellous, isn't it, really? So convenient."

"Prudence, I think that is a wonderful idea. Though I am not sure you will get there today. The weather is still awful."

***

And awful, it remained. With half our group in hospital, Frederico and I stranded in Oysterhaven, and the rain and wind competing for who could manage the most damage, there would be no 'Walkers' walk this Saturday. I texted everyone, though, just to confirm.

I also called Sam at the Cottage Hospital to let her know that I wouldn't be able to complete my regular round of patient visits. This naturally led to a conversation about how Barbara and Avril were doing and the result of the tests.

Before Sam could do the big reveal, I had to get in first.

"I think you will find it's the rhubarb." I was now sure that was the link, as it was the only pot I bought, so must have been the one that the 'Baron' had eaten.

"As I was just about to say, the tests confirm it was oxalic acid. Rhubarb leaves are poisonous and full of the stuff. You are quite the sleuth these days, aren't you? Maybe you should consider a career change?"

"Oh, I have no desire to be a police officer. I don't like the uniforms, and it's way too dangerous. Maybe Sherlock Holmes?"

"Hmm, does that make me Dr Watson?" Sam suddenly deepened her voice and in a clipped upper-class accent continued, "Well, my dear Sherlock, tally-ho! Must dash, patients to cure, and all that."

I loved Sam; she had such a glorious sense of humour. I was just about to call Zuzu when the main vicarage phone rang in the hall. Forgetting I wasn't at home, I ran to answer it. But Prudence, surprisingly spritely for her age, got there first.

My journey no longer required, I turned to walk back to the kitchen.

There was a gasp from behind me.

I rewound to see a visibly shaken Prudence handing me the receiver.

In a trembling voice, she muttered. "It's the police!"

My heart sank.

I took the phone.

"Yes, it's Reverend Ward here. How can I help?"

"Reverend. I am sorry to report that Professor Helen Linden has been found dead in her home. The vicarage number was on her noticeboard. I imagine she is a member of your parish? Would you know whom we should contact as next of kin?"

Professor Linden is dead!

"I'm sorry, Officer, I'm just a guest. The parish priest is in hospital. But I will ask around and get back to you if I learn anything. May I ask how she died?"

"We are not sure of the exact cause at present. Not until the autopsy. But early indications are that she may have been poisoned."

***

I called Sam at the hospital again straight away. She found the news of Helen Linden's death very interesting, from a clinical point of view.

"Death from rhubarb poisoning is extremely rare. Ingesting the leaves can make one very ill and all the symptoms exhibited by those in the hospital fit that diagnosis, and the tests bear that out, but death? Unless she had an underlying health condition like Reverend Cattermole..." I could practically hear the gears working in Sam's brain down the phone. "The amounts of oxalic acid were not enough to... By the way, I was just on a call to the General and they have moved Cattermole out of ICU. He's back on Seacole Ward."

"Oh, that is marvellous news! Perhaps, if the weather lets up, I will visit him and Maureen before heading back to the Island. Any news on the Inspector?"

"I heard he is doing extremely well and should be discharged soon. They were way ahead of us in thinking it was possibly oxalic acid. The team could get the charcoal treatment started quickly. He will be back protecting us from thieves and murderers real soon."

"Talking of murderers." I dropped my voice to a whisper and cupped the mouthpiece of the phone with my hand. "I thought this was just an awful accident, but now one of us is dead. Do you think there is any chance this was deliberate?"

"Jess, with poison, there is always the chance it was deliberate. Let's see what the autopsy report says before we make wild accusations. Okay? This is Wesberrey, not 'Midsomer Murders'. Food poisoning happens, and it's more likely a tragic but innocent mistake."

Sam was right, of course, but my spidey senses were tingling (I watched way too many cartoons as a kid). Maybe I have a psychic gift after all. The feeling that something was wrong was very strong, and as Uncle Ben said at the start of every Saturday morning episode of Spiderman 'with great power comes great responsibility'.

I need to find out who killed Helen Linden.

***

The wind still howled outside, and the rain showed no sign of abating. Despite my keenness to get to the bottom of this mystery, my first duty was to look after Prudence, who was visibly in shock at the news. A cup of sweet tea would do the trick and a warm blanket. I remembered seeing a blue tartan one in the lounge the night before.

"Right, you sit here by the fire, Mrs Beckworth. Let me get you some tea." I wrapped her up in the blanket and grabbed a nearby footstool to raise her feet. I noticed she had shoes on and thought she would be more comfortable in slippers. "Can I fetch anything for you? Do you want to take off your shoes? I can help?"

"No, you're alright, dear. I put my shoes on when I get up. If I take them off now, I will never get them back on when we go to the hospital. My feet swell so much, see…" Prudence pointed down to her thick ankles.

"Well, just tea it is, then. And afterwards, I'll phone Seacole Ward to check up on Richard and Maureen. Make sure they are up to visitors today. If the weather keeps on, we will get a taxi."

"Bless you, Reverend. Please, can you call Conrad and tell him the news? I don't want him finding out from the police."

***

"Don't worry about a taxi, Reverend. I will drive you both to the hospital. I should have been up to see old Cattermole already. That man's been like a brother to me over the years. Just the farm takes up so much of my time. It's why I joined the 'Otters' to be honest with you. It was his baby, and I felt it was my duty to support him. And it was a splendid way to meet the ladies, you know."

Conrad had driven over within minutes of ending our call. The farm was obviously close by. Less than an hour after hearing about the professor's untimely death, the eclectic gathering of Frederico, Prudence, Conrad, and I were making small talk on the comfy chairs and sofas in the vicarage lounge.

"I suppose you knew Helen Linden well then as she was an 'Otter' before her defection to the 'Strollers'."

"Yes, her decision rocked the association. Helen had been such a force. I have never known a woman, or a man, for that matter, so committed to rambling. She walked fast. Really fast. Legs like a gazelle. Lean. Pure muscle. Shapely rump, though. Looked mighty fine in her khaki shorts. Had no qualms about picking up the rear, if you know what I mean." Conrad executed a pantomime stage wink straight out of a 'Carry on' movie from the Sixties. "No 'in' there, though, regrettably. Not from the want of trying, if you get my drift?"

"Conrad! Reverend, I apologise for my son's brutish remarks. I taught him better than this." Prudence cast a disapproving glare at her son, who appeared to shrink in his chair.

"Mother, I merely meant it was a waste of fine breeding stock. Even this Latino bull wouldn't have caught her eye." Conrad's hands pointed to Frederico. "If you take my meaning, Reverend Ward."

"There's no need to soil her reputation just because she spurned your attentions. The poor soul is dead!" Prudence fussed with her blanket and lifted herself up. "I think it's time we set off to the General. No good all of us sitting around here. Look to the living, eh?"

As Prudence got to her feet, we all instinctively rose. The conversation had ended, and it was a welcome relief on one level to move away from Conrad's archaic, sexist remarks. However, I sensed he had more to tell me about Helen Linden. Unpleasant a prospect as it seemed, I would need to talk to Conrad without his mother present.

Dog-Collared Harlot

Seacole Ward was bright and airy with enormous windows giving the patients, staff and visitors a glorious panoramic view of the town's roundabouts, car parks, shopping centre and office blocks. A grey vista on the best of days. With only two visitors allowed at each bedside, we agreed to divide ourselves up to sit beside Reverend Cattermole and Maureen, and swap after about twenty minutes. Frederico and I went to see Judith's cousin first.

"Ooh, Vicar. So very nice of you to pop by again. The nurses told me you were here the other night. Good to see the Reverend Cattermole out of ICU and back on the ward. I think they were all a little worried about him. But the staff here have been brilliant. Can't fault them at all. The great NHS, eh?" Maureen was wearing a knitted mint green bed jacket that she drew close to her chest as she spoke. "Terrible news about Helen, though. Can't have been Judith's jam, surely Vicar? Eh? Or my rhubarb? I've been growing it for years. Judith is a stickler for hygiene. I just can't see it myself, Vicar. Just doesn't seem real."

"I know what you mean, Maureen. It must just be a mistake. Perhaps some leaves got into the maslin pan. I imagine that's easy to do if you're distracted or..."

Maureen shook her head. "Vicar, I highly doubt it. My stalks are bright pink. The leaves are a pale green. That's the beauty of growing them in the dark. Makes them much sweeter. And the leaves are smaller. You would need tons to have any effect. No, I think somebody had to add them deliberately. Chopped up very fine. Whoever did this would need to blend them in well. I really can't see how it was accidental." Maureen stopped talking suddenly. The magnitude of her words struck home. "Judith would never, never in a million years, do anything to hurt anyone. She is the sweetest, kindest person…" Her voice trailed off.

Maureen reached for a tissue from the box on the wooden pedestal beside her bed. I thought I should change the conversation, so remarked on the beautiful bouquet also on the pedestal.

"Lovely blooms." I stood up to take a closer look. I have never really had a great sense of smell, but for some reason, I always pretend to sniff the flower heads. Wouldn't be able to separate a dahlia from a peony from their scent, but they were beautiful. Dark red roses with a dash of mimosa. Not quite what I would expect in a hospital. I noticed there was a card, but no name. "Secret admirer, eh?"

"No, Vicar. Just a friend." Maureen seemed ruffled. "Actually, Vicar, as you are standing, can you get me some fresh water? The jug is on the bedside table there. I hate to bother the nurses."

"Of course. Do you need anything else? Frederico could run to the shop in the foyer."

"No need to trouble on my account," she huffed.

Frederico leapt at the chance for freedom. "No, please, er, Maureen? I am happy to get something. Even from the town, perhaps?" His puppy-dog eyes pleaded with her. "I could do with the walk and the air. I dislike hospitals and I want to be, er, vantajoso, useful."

Maureen stiffened slightly before charitably agreeing that some fresh magazines and grapes, even chocolate, would be nice. Once Frederico had left, she slipped out of her bed and made herself comfortable in the high-back chair on the right-hand side of the bed.

"He seems a lovely man. Foreign, though. Good teeth."

"Yes, he's from Brazil. I think he's glad to be rid of me for a little while. The storm trapped us here last night. He had an interview, you see, at the Uni…"

"All very nice, I'm sure, Vicar. But I'm not accustomed to entertaining strange men at my bedside. Not without the proper introductions." She bristled. "Must have slipped your mind. Far more juicy topics of conversation to engage in. Easy to forget the niceties, even for a member of the clergy."

Oh my! What a faux pas. In my desire to get a few more clues on the mystery, I had completely forgotten that Frederico was not at the meeting on Tuesday. He and Maureen had never met and now this stranger is sitting at her bedside in the hospital. No woman wants to be presented to a handsome man in her nightie with no makeup. This explained her off-hand behaviour. I wondered what Frederico was thinking about all this madness. He has said virtually nothing all day and just trotted along with my plans like a well-trained chihuahua.

I really hoped the ferry would be operating again soon.

A quick look out of the vast sheets of glass that lined the ward brightened my mood. There were clear skies on the horizon. With any luck, we would return to Wesberrey that evening and back to some sense of normality. I felt I was losing my mind a little.

"Maureen, I am so terribly sorry for any impropriety."

"Hmm, a fancy word for being just plain rude. You know, Audrey Matthews warned us about you, Vicar." Maureen reached into the pedestal drawer and pulled out a crochet hook and a ball of rainbow yarn. "Judith told her she was being unfair." Waving the needle in my direction, she added. "Audrey can be very protective of her Stanley. He had quite an eye for the ladies, but once he settled down with Audrey…" Leaning forward, Maureen's eyes fixed on mine. "Audrey isn't one for sharing, Vicar. Do you understand? Stanley may be all starry-eyed about this new female Father Brown that goes about sticking her nose into everyone's business. Must seem very glamorous; going around unearthing secrets, solving murders, being where you're not wanted. You just leave him alone. Do you understand? We're on to you, Reverend Jessamy Ward."

So that is what the school secretary has against me. She thinks I'm after her man!

"Maureen, I assure you. I am not out to steal anyone's husband, and certainly not Stanley Matthews!" I almost laughed at the absurd suggestion but muffled it by clenching my lips together.

"I guess he's not good enough for you when you can have some Argentine beefcake." I wanted to correct her that Frederico was Brazilian but decided this wasn't the time to be pedantic. Not that Maureen stopped to take a breath. "We aren't fooled by that dog collar. You're a single woman. And a woman has needs. Now, if you don't mind, this hat isn't going to make itself."

Speechless and to be honest, shocked, I bowed and went over to the safer territory around Reverend Cattermole's bed at the opposite end of the ward. Swapping seats with Prudence, I watched as the Beckworths greeted Miss Sykes. Maybe I was being paranoid, but I suspected, from the animated glances across at me every few seconds, that their conversation was largely about the dog-collared harlot of Wesberrey.

I prayed that Frederico would come back soon. Funny how travelling home with him now seemed a much more attractive proposition than staying here pulling out the daggers from my back.

Something Fishy

Never had the familiar sight of Bob McGuire and his ferry chugging into port been so welcome. Fortunately, the channel was as calm as a mirror. I wasn't sure I could have taken a choppy crossing. There had been enough drama for one day.

Frederico and I barely spoke on our journey back to the island. For an intelligent man, he was very tenacious in thought. He centred the small amount of conversation we had on my sister and his quest to win her back. He sounded like a broken record.

We bid farewell outside the 'Cat and Fiddle' and I rode 'Cilla' back home. When I reached Cliff View, I stopped to take a breath before entering the house. The sun was settling herself in her bed for the night, and the world around me was finally calm. The trees were still, and there were no signs of the storm that had battered the island for the last twenty-four hours. Birds were sharing their evensong, and all other creatures listened in a joint communion of thanksgiving. It was as if Mother Nature had opened the windows to let some air in. Everything was pure again.

Except it wasn't. I knew Helen Linden had been murdered. I knew it so deep in my core there was no shaking it. I had to speak to more people who knew her, and I needed to speak with Judith.

It was getting late and my body ached to get back inside the warmth of the vicarage, to see my family and feel at home.

A welcome fluffy form was sitting on the doorstep.

"Hey there, Hugo. You're the only man I want in my life right now. Here, give me a hug." I bent down to scoop him up, only to send him darting off to the back of the house and the graveyard beyond. "Great! Thanks for the vote of confidence." I straightened up and put my key in the latch.

There was a sudden and unmistakable sound of smashing glass.

My fish!

I walked in to find a dazed Luke standing in the middle of the hallway with blood dripping from his right hand.

"I'm so sorry, Aunt Jess. I was just looking at your collection... erm, I was holding one up to look at the colours in the light. It was so cool. Blues and greens and... and, then I heard you at the door and, well, I must have tripped on the way back to the sideboard because I fell and it shattered when I hit the ground. I'm so sorry."

"Luke, It's no big deal. You've hurt yourself. Come to the kitchen. I hope it wasn't the speckled fish with the black eyes, that's my favourite." I cast Luke a quick glance from the corner of my eye and his anguished look confirmed that it was. "It's okay. Don't worry. It only cost me a few pence at the Stepney 'Bring 'n' Buy'."

Alerted by the sounds of glass and chaos, Mum and Rosie soon joined us in the kitchen, and I handed Luke over to his mother to nurse him. Mum put on the kettle, and within a few minutes, order was restored.

I took a dustpan and brush into the morning room to clean up. Blue and green glass shards covered the floor. Luke was very lucky not to have got a splinter in his eye. I swept the fishy remains into a pile and then onto the pan. The breaks were clean. Maybe the poor thing could be glued back together. If only we could do that with people.

I sat motionless in the middle of the rug.

What a day!

I closed my eyes, but I couldn't rest. I had a sermon to prepare for tomorrow and my mind was buzzing with thoughts of my conversations with Maureen, Frederico, Conrad, Zuzu, and Dave. I couldn't find peace. The wind outside may have died, but it was still whirling around my head, looking to make sense of the past few days. The broken fish was the least of my concerns. If only I could just visualise Helen's killer like last time. This was more than a simple case of poisoning now. I was sure of it. Maybe, if I just wrote something down and got it out of my head.

I took a detour on my return to the kitchen to sit for a while at my desk. Luke was in the best hands, and they didn't need the spinster aunt fussing around making everything worse. I took my notepad and turned it to a fresh page. In black biro I wrote Helen Linden's name in the centre and circled it several times. Then I wrote above it *'Who killed…'* and added a large question mark below. I closed my eyes again, and placing both my hands palms down on the notepad, I thought about this question over and over and over again. *Who killed Helen Linden? Who killed Helen Linden?* I tried to shut out all other thoughts, but the conversation with Maureen refused to budge. Why is she so bothered about the harlot priest when she has a love interest of her own? And what is it about women pulling other women down? *Who killed Helen Linden?* Why on earth would anyone feel threatened by me? Since when has a dog collar been sexy?

Who killed Helen Linden?

Why couldn't I see anything? I wasn't sure who I was asking anymore. God? The Goddess of the Triple Wells? My subconscious? Obviously, whoever or whatever it was, wasn't listening.

This was a complete waste of time. I needed to prepare for tomorrow.

Two masses in two separate parishes where several inhabitants are recovering from a poison attack. Now one of them has died, I needed to make the most of the opportunities this presented for the homily. It was Passion Sunday. The gospel would be the raising of Lazarus. The sermon should be easy to write. At times like this, it is important to think about the power of hope and love. That in Jesus we can find eternal life. Easy though the theme may be, it still needed writing; and the distracting scent of crushed garlic and rosemary told me Mum was preparing chicken for dinner.

***

"So, this thing between Zuzu and the 'Baron' is getting serious then? Do you think she'll be moving out soon?" Rosie refilled her glass with water from the jug and took a sip. "And where does that leave Frederico? Surely he's got the message by now?"

I could see Mum was tutting under her breath. Her opinion of my older sister's relationships was never a welcome addition to a conversation, and I knew she was trying to suppress any negative comments. As she would always say, if you can't say something nice, then say nothing at all.

I thought Rosie's question needed an informed response. "After spending twenty-four hours with Frederico, I understand why Zuzu would be, er, uncomfortable in that relationship. However, I really think she cares deeply for Dave. You didn't see her in the hospital. I think she believes that this one is worth the effort."

"Exactly that!" Mum swallowed her last mouthful of braised carrot. "Zuzu has never put in any effort! Love is hard work. You need to stand firm through the hard times. It's not all red roses and violins."

Red roses.

"Mum, can I ask your advice on this goddess thing?" I could feel Rosie and Luke's incredulous eyes bearing into me. My mother, in contrast, just put down her knife and fork and readied herself for a deep conversation. "I mean, not that I am giving any of it any credence but —"

"Jess, have you had another vision?" Mum stretched out her hand. Her fingertips briefly stroked the back of my right hand before she awkwardly removed them and placed her hand back on the table in front of her.

"No. And that's the problem! I thought, I mean, I believe in prayer, of course. And I often meditate. I like the stillness. I need the space it offers to clarify my thoughts. But recently I can't seem to even do that. So I thought, what if I could deliberately channel it all? You know, get focus. Test it out, I guess. If there is a way to control these insights and use them to help…"

"Track down poisoners?" Mum had that look on her face. The one I knew well as a child. A look that said: 'Don't dare even think about doing that!' "Jess, to poison someone requires malice aforethought. Intention. They planned it. If someone can plot the death of another, then you should stay as far away from them as possible. Gift or no gift."

"So, does that mean you won't help me?" I could feel my teenage self rising inside. "I'll ask Aunt Cindy then, or Pamela. She would love to teach me."

Now I recognised a very different look on my mother's face. One I had also seen many times before. Often during my time as a petulant teenager, and again when I told her I was giving up my dream of being an actress to enter the seminary. It was the look of a thousand sorrows, one of crushing betrayal.

"Mum, I'm sorry. It's just that you never really talked about this side of your life after we left the Island. I didn't realise you believed in all this. I'm really not sure that I do, or that I can, but I can't carry on as before. Something has shifted, and I need to work it out. Will you help me?"

"Hmm, I knew this would happen once you came back here. You changed after visiting the well for Imbolc. If it's really what you want, I will speak to Pam." Mum started muttering to herself, her eyes darting around as she pieced her thoughts together. "It was the equinox last week, and it's not a full moon 'til the eighth, but I'm sure if we all gather we can help you connect. We have Rosie this time too. Two generations of sisters will be extremely powerful."

"If we can drag Zuzu back from playing nursemaid." Rosie chirped. "Though I really enjoyed equinox. I think Pam and Cindy are so cool."

"Whoa, hold on there, little Sis. What do you mean? Did you all meet up and cast runes and stuff last week without me? I thought it was 'just a 'drink'!" I made a point of doing 'bunny ears' when I said the word 'drink'.

Secrets and lies!

"You had your 'Walker's Workout'! Mum made reciprocal 'bunny ears'. "And we don't cast runes, well not all of us." Her mood had lifted. "If you must know, we just joined hands around Pam's dining table and said a few words over some prawn cocktails. And the prawns hadn't thawed properly, so the starter became a glass of white wine and a slice of wholemeal toast."

"Without the crusts! Don't forget Aunt Pam cut off all the crusts."

Mum and Rosie fell about laughing. I cast an enquiring eye over to Luke.

"Don't look at me!" He replied. "I was stuck in the shed with Uncle Byron most of the evening. I now know more than I will ever need to about double O standard gauges."

Passion Sunday part one

The sun-filled calm following the storm brought a healthy congregation to St. Bridget's. The story of Lazarus usually generates a lively post-service conversation in the hall afterwards, but this morning, without Barbara's catering to hold them, most of my parishioners slipped away as quickly as they considered it polite to do so. I got the chance, though, to have a quick word with Judith and Keith.

"Vicar, everyone is saying it's my jam! It will ruin me! It wasn't, I assure you. How could it be? I am so careful. Only Keith and I have access to our kitchen. I don't even let Maureen in when she visits. In fact, sometimes I lock myself away if a batch is cooking." As she spoke, Judith maintained a watchful eye on everyone else in the hall, like a meerkat on sentry duty. Her nerves were beyond frazzled. "She sells them back on her farm, you see. Keith has to entertain her, poor thing. Don't you, Love? And I know how easily bored she is." Judith lovingly stroked Keith's arm. "We may be cousins, but we have such different temperaments. Maureen is moody. Isn't she?"

Keith, seemingly oblivious to his wife's state of extreme agitation, had been casting his eye over the last of Rosemary's custard tarts but snapped back at his wife's question.

"No one could equal you, my dear. She's but a pale imitation. Maureen can be demanding. Sometimes my darling Judith works through the night to prepare a batch of jam for her farm shop and barely gets a thank you in return. But the people of Oysterhaven love it." In contrast to Judith's angular features, Keith's were fairly nondescript. Average height. Average build. In fact, it was almost as if he wore a 'Mr Average' mask to avoid anyone's closer scrutiny. I half expected him to vanish into a phone box to don a mask and something with more lycra. Instead, less dramatic but infinitely more endearing, he remained stoically by his wife's side. "Don't worry, dear, I am sure that they will soon forget all of this. We'll change the labels or something. People move on, don't they, Reverend Ward?"

"I agree. Once they know the details, people will be very forgiving." I wanted to steer the conversation back on track. "So, no one else would have had access to the jam during processing?"

"Not a soul, Vicar. That is why I don't understand how it's happened." The strain had etched fresh lines on Judith's weary face. I doubt she had had much sleep. "PC Taylor took a few jars for testing. He said to expect a visit from the council's food standards officer. They could shut us down completely."

"I'm sure it won't come to that. I've heard they think it was the rhubarb jam." Hoping to show a sign of solidarity with the couple, I added, "I'm kind of sorry that I didn't get to taste any. My sister gave it to the Inspector. Admittedly, he is now in hospital, but I hear it was divine."

"And deadly, Vicar, and deadly." Judith sobbed into a paper napkin. Keith put his arm around his wife and made their apologies.

As Keith ushered his wife away, Phil took his opportunity to catch a quick word before I dashed to the ferry.

"They're letting Barbara 'ome this afternoon, Vicar. I know you have back-to-back masses and will probably need a break, but would you be happy to visit 'er this afternoon? You know 'ow she worries about everything. Put 'er mind at rest. Let 'er know you're fine without her."

"Of course, Phil. I will grab some of those amazing cakes from the 'Whistle Stop' Cafe on my way back. Theirs are the only ones to come close to Barbara's own magnificent creations."

"That would be lovely, just nothing with coconut. She hates coconut. Or rhubarb!" He tried to laugh, but it was too soon, too raw.

"Phil, you care a lot for Barbara, don't you? You have been up at the hospital every day. Several times a day."

"She is my world, Vicar. I 'ave no idea what I would do without her. This poisoning thing has scared me so much. I'm a man. It's my job to fix stuff. That's what I do, and I was powerless. I couldn't fix this." His silver-blue eyes brimmed with tears. I could see he was biting his lip to hold them back.

"Phil, have you ever told her how you feel?"

"Me? What, tell Barbara? And ruin our friendship? She's a beautiful woman. A genuine woman. Womanly in all the right ways. She deserves the best. The absolute best. What would she want with a common verger?"

"There is nothing common about you, Phil. Such a womanly woman needs a handsome, loving caretaker." I tried to maintain eye contact, but Phil's eyes were cast towards the ground. I pressed on. "A strong man who gives to his community. Puts others before himself and owns the only pub on the island! Not that Barbara would be in any way mercenary, but Phil, you really are quite the catch! And she adores you. You must be the only person who can't see it!"

"Vicar, even if what you say is true that boat sailed long ago. Love is for the young. We are far too old for that sort of thing at our age."

"Love is ageless and the greatest gift we have from God. What greater comfort is there than to find someone you can grow old with? Why don't you think about it, eh?"

Phil wrapped his bear-like arms around me and finally fixed me with his eyes as he pulled back. "You are a wonderful woman, Vicar." I resisted the urge to ask if I was also a womanly woman, whatever that meant, as it would have spoiled a very tender moment.

"Right, well. I have to dash. Text me when Barbara is home, and if you need more alone time with her, just let me know. Otherwise, I'll be round for tea and cake later."

***

When I arrived at the port, the harbour was teeming with dozens of calico and tortoise-shell blobs of fur. The fishing boats had deposited their first morning catch in days and the Island's wild cat colony was making the most of the remains. I knew they weren't starving. I had designated Luke as chief cat feeder shortly after he arrived, and the donations from the local community and other visitors to the island meant we have enough tins of salmon and tuna chunks to feed this fluffy army for the next two years.

As always, Bob McGuire was waiting to welcome me onto his ferry.

"Double shift today, Vicar. I think you'll find the people at St. Mildred's are a peculiar breed."

"In my experience, Bob, people are the same everywhere. We're all peculiar."

"If you say so, Vicar. Terrible business, though, all this. I liked Professor Linden. Can't believe it. She was such a robust woman. She used to leave the 'Walkers' and all the others for dust every year. I guess her loss will be someone else's gain, eh? And the news will bring more tourists for the Easter weekend. Nothing like a bit of scandal to draw in the visitors."

"Er, yes, I suppose so. You knew Helen Linden well then?"

"As well as I know any of them. Mandy is always on at me to join her precious walking group. Says I need to be more active, but there are some people I don't want to hang around with, and I can't stand hypocrites. They think I don't have eyes and ears."

Bob may prove to be a man of valuable insight. What did he mean? What had he seen and heard? "Do you have anyone in mind when you say that?" I asked. "They all seem such lovely people to me."

"Yep, I guess they all scrub up clean when you're around, eh? But I hear too much. I see even more. Take Keith Hudson. One skinny blonde isn't enough for him. Having it away with his wife's near-identical cousin is kinda creepy, if you ask me, Vicar."

Keith and Maureen are having an affair! Did he send the red roses? Oh my! It was appalling. I mean, I'm not easily shocked, but... poor Judith! Though that would explain Maureen's change of mood when I mentioned the flowers. Keith? What a snake!

"Adultery is a sin. They are taking a risk openly displaying their relationship on a ferry. Someone could see — "

"Oh, *someone* sees. I'm like wallpaper. They hide behind that funnel there and think they're invisible. Sometimes it pains my eyes to watch. Especially when it's raining and they think everyone is below deck. People get a thrill out of that kind of thing, I suppose. The risk. It adds to the thrill. Folks have affairs because they need excitement, I guess. I don't get it myself. But then I still live in the same house I grew up in, with my sister and her kids for company, so what do I know? I like routine. I like to come and go with the tide, and I am content with my quiet life."

Bob suddenly fascinated me. The trusty ferryman, never leaving this island except to run the course to and from the mainland multiple times a day. "Did you never want to marry?"

"Oh, I loved a girl once. She had such cute freckles and the sweetest pigtails, but she left years ago."

A faint memory of my little sister Rosie complaining of having her pigtails tugged by a certain young Bob McGuire shot across my mind. Was Bob carrying a torch for my baby sister? Since primary school! How sweet and, at the same time, how pathetic.

I looked to gauge if his memory of love had stirred anything, but his eyes remained focused on the port ahead. *Amor.* Its tendrils run deep within us all. Passion causes us to act as if we were mad. Romance makes us fools. Love can make us both blissfully happy and

90

desperately sad. It can drive us on or halt us in our tracks, and maybe it could even cause someone to add rhubarb leaves to a pot of jam.

So, Judith and Maureen were rivals in love and rivals in the Walkathon. But they seemed so chummy at the meeting? Maybe the culinary addition of rhubarb leaves to the maslin pot was not an accidental oversight. If the poisonings were deliberate, was Maureen the target? If so, which one of the Hudsons did it? Did Judith want revenge on her cousin? Or maybe Keith had wanted to end his extra-marital relationship, and Maureen wasn't leaving quietly? Was his lover planning to tell her cousin? If so, Keith might want to warn her off, incapacitate her for a while, until she saw sense. Or was this designed to hurt Judith? As she said, the scandal could ruin her.

The ferry bounced off the rubber tyres of the quayside, and Bob left his station to begin the docking procedure. Left alone with my thoughts, I questioned if that was why I had seen that peculiar parade of faces when I tried to focus on Judith? Recalling the sequence as it played out in my mind, I saw Judith, then Keith, then Maureen. My subconscious, or my gift, had been trying to tell me something. I just hadn't been open enough to listen. If Keith or Judith set out to hurt Maureen, then Helen Linden and the others were all just innocent victims of a sordid ménage à trois.

Passion Sunday Part Two

A rmed with this fresh information, I journeyed on to St. Mildred's with a renewed sense of excitement and trepidation. If Keith deliberately added the rhubarb leaves to the jam to get back at Maureen, or if Judith did it to harm her rival, how did those actions lead to Helen Linden's death? Was she, tragically, like the other people affected, mere collateral damage? For Keith, who was not at the meeting in the hall, there was no way of knowing which jar Maureen would take. A special one 'just' for her would make his wife suspicious once the source of the poisoning came out. If it were Judith, it would make sense to disguise Maureen's poisoning amongst a few others. That way it would look more like an accident. Such a plan, though, ran the genuine risk of destroying her business. Surely there were better ways of getting back at a cheating cousin? It was a perilous strategy. But then I suppose, as Frederico has said, all things are fair in love and war.

These explanations, though, failed to answer the main conundrum of who killed Helen Linden. How could it have been the rhubarb? Everyone seemed to agree that she was über fit. Maureen and the others, with the obvious exception of Reverend Cattermole, had been very ill, but they were seemingly never in any *real* danger. Other underlying health conditions complicated Richard Cattermole's condition, but even *he* was now on the road to recovery. Helen must have received a message about the poisoning. An intelligent woman like her would seek medical help if she experienced any symptoms. Wouldn't she?

Maybe Helen didn't know! Eunice only said that she had called the 'Otters'. I forgot Helen was now a 'Stroller'. Eunice must feel awful that she didn't alert Helen to the danger. What with all the rivalry and feelings of betrayal over her defection, they were clearly still friends. I had seen them chatting after the meeting. Thank heaven for small mercies. What if her last words to her old friend had been 'Traitor!'? How terrible. Hopefully, I would have some time after mass to talk to Eunice and offer my support.

I arrived at the, now familiar, vicarage. Conrad was standing on the threshold, dressed in his Sunday best, waiting to greet me.

"Reverend Ward! I can't believe it was only yesterday that you were here last. I say, you are looking mighty fine. I see you sport a slight touch of Sunday rouge. It suits you." Conrad held out his arm as if he were about to escort me into the ball. I wasn't sure what to do. I'm certain he was being gallant in the most innocent way, but it didn't seem appropriate. I declined with a smile.

"Thank you, Conrad, but I know the way. How is your mother this morning? I imagine yesterday's news and all the drama took its toll."

"Oh, Mother is as strong as an ox. Takes more than a suspicious death to derail her from her duties. She's been up from before light preparing the church for you. News has spread that we are to have a celebrity in our midst. The church was full half an hour ago!"

"I'm not a celebrity!" I laughed.

"You are infamous around here, Reverend."

"Not as the dog-collared harlot, I hope," I muttered to myself.

"Did I hear you say harlot? Why ever would anyone say that about you? Oh, you must mean Maureen. Bitter woman. No one pays any mind to what she says. Though, if you were, that would make my quest a darn sight more promising." He winked. A part of me deep inside shuddered at the thought of being Conrad's latest conquest. "You are in the 'Stourchestershire Times' a lot. They love you and all your detecting. Is that even a word? No mind, the service begins soon." Conrad pulled an elegant pocket watch on a chain from his tweed vest. "In ten minutes, to be precise. I'll leave you to it. Toodle pip!"

Toodle pip? Did he really just say toodle pip?

Prudence was waiting for me at the door of the sacristy.

"Take all the time you need, Reverend. It's a full house, but I'm sure you'll be fine. Just give the organist the nod in the mirror here, and he'll begin the first hymn."

"Thank you, Prudence. I will see you on the other side."

She pressed my hands together in hers and curtsied slightly. I couldn't imagine how the bullish Conrad was the fruit of this gentle soul.

***

Second time around my Lazarus sermon lacked the freshness it had earlier that morning, but the St. Mildred's congregation seemed happy enough. They packed the adjacent village hall afterwards, all keen to shake my hand and offer their best wishes for Reverend Cattermole. Conrad brought me over a cup of milky tea in a striking yellow 'beryl ware' cup and saucer. I had a green set of the same crockery back at St. Bridget's. There was probably a set in every church hall across England. Yellow was rare though — they were mostly blue or green.

"Don't buy it," Conrad whispered in my ear, offering me a small plate of chocolate digestives.

"Buy what?"

"This outpouring of best wishes for Reverend Cattermole. I doubt most of them even know who he is! They're here for the beautiful lady vicar, trust me."

I smiled. In my head, though, I was highly amused. Beautiful? Me? It's just a bit of blusher! Conrad was definitely persistent.

I spotted a familiar face out of the corner of my eye. It was the tall, blond figure of Leo Peasbody, the local undertaker, and Dr Sam's occasional bedfellow. I decided that a handshake was in order and pushed my way through the packed hall.

"Mr Peasbody, so nice to see you again." I wanted to ask how his work was going, but that seemed inappropriate given his occupation, so I continued with a general enquiry about his health. "How have you been? Fortunately, we haven't had need of your services on Wesberrey for a few months now."

"Indeed, it has been quiet there of late. Which is a wonderful thing, of course, for its inhabitants, not so great for trade."

"I understand. We are in similar businesses. Not a lot of weddings for me at the moment, but come the summer... Do you know who is helping with Professor Linden's funeral?"

"I am awaiting instructions from the county coroner. I understand she has no immediate kin, so it will probably be a small affair."

"That's really sad. But I think there will be many who will want to show their respects. Helen was a keen rambler and a university professor. Her colleagues and students will all want to mark her passing, I expect."

"Maybe. I'm sorry, Reverend Ward, but I don't have any details. Erm, do you mind if I ask after Dr Hawthorne? Is she well?"

"Sam? Oh, yes. Yes, she is. These poisonings have been keeping her busy this past week. You know, perhaps you should visit sometime other than for a funeral. What about over the Easter break? Hard to believe that it's just two weeks away now. There's the 'Walkathon' and all the activities that run alongside it. A lovely way to bring the community together on Easter Saturday. I'm looking forward to it. Back in London, it was just another day to go shopping and pay over the odds for chocolate eggs."

"Well, I will do my best to be there. Hopefully, I won't be working."

"Yes, hopefully. Oh, and if Reverend Cattermole isn't well enough for Helen's funeral, I am more than happy to conduct the service."

"How do you know she wasn't a pagan?"

I turned to find Eunice Drinkwater's square face peering over my left shoulder.

"I'm sorry. Was she? I just assumed. Was she not a member of this parish?"

"She was a member of the 'Otters'. You can do one without the other. Helen didn't believe in God, but she loved to walk. She taught that the church is a patriarchal construct that suppresses women. She only came to the meeting last week to view the lady vicar with the pagan aunts."

"I'm sorry if I disappointed her, but I don't share my family's beliefs." Uttering that public denial made my private heart pang a bit.

"That's a shame, because Helen thought it was fascinating. She wanted to study your family history as part of her next research project on the matriarchal goddess tradition. But I suppose that doesn't matter now as she's..." Eunice's fierce expression crumbled. "Excuse me. I need to be elsewhere."

"Eunice, could I pop over sometime? Maybe tomorrow, or later in the week?" I called after her. "To talk to you about Helen. You seem to be the only one who really knew her, and I want to work with Mr Peasbody here to ensure she has an appropriate sendoff."

Eunice stopped and turned. Slowly.

"Really, you would want to talk to me? I... I'm not sure. Call me. You have my number. This is all very... I really must go."

Eunice wiped her eyes on the sleeve of her jacket and barged her way out of the hall.

Moving Forward

I stopped by the 'Whistle Stop' cafe to pick up some lemon drizzle cake for Barbara. I had a few minutes to spare before the next ferry back, so I ordered an almond milk latte with a vanilla shot to take away. Wesberrey needs a wonderful coffee shop like this, I thought as I settled myself on one of the bar stools facing out the window across to the port. I had an excellent view of the ferry. Though the sun blazed bright, it remained perishingly cold outside. It was far more beneficial to my soul to view the landscape of screeching seagulls and bustling coastal warehouses from the comfort of the shop's interior.

My thoughts turned to Eunice. Obviously there was a lot of residual pain from her friendship with Helen. The charge of 'Traitor' ran deeper than a mere defection to a rival walking group. Whether or not Helen was religious, I wanted to make sure she had a good send-off, and Eunice appeared to know her better than most.

I sat cradling the large porcelain mug in both hands and breathed in deeply. There really is nothing like the smell of freshly roasted coffee. I had missed it. Back in London, there are coffee houses on every corner. Securing a good cup of java was never a problem. The city of Stourchester was well catered for in the 'grab a quick expresso' department, with several chain and independent coffee houses, but this was really the only spot in Oysterhaven. Wesberrey was a coffee desert. I am sure they do a lovely French roast at 'The Old School House' restaurant, but their prices are way beyond the means of a clergywoman. The 'Cat and Fiddle' has an old filter coffee machine, but nowhere can create the magic that is a frothy latte or cappuccino. My mind turned to ideas for the old book shop that my family was to inherit from Violet Smith. Perhaps we could open a coffee shop? That would be a wonderful idea. But who would run it? Mum? Zuzu? No, I couldn't see that working. Rosie? Maybe. I made a mental note to suggest it at dinner that evening.

***

"Funnily enough, I was thinking the same thing." Rosie passed the gravy to her son. "But I didn't want to upset Mum by discussing it. Luke and I could move into the cottage on Love Lane and take over the shop."

"Yeah," Luke chimed in. "From what I can see through the window, I think there is enough space in the back room for some gaming PCs and stuff. We could make the entire thing more twenty-first century." This was the most animated I had ever seen my nephew. "We would need to invest in the best equipment. Proper chairs and all the right consoles and headphones and so on. And internet. It's surprisingly good on the island, considering you don't even have cars."

"Yes, that would be the huge mast at the back of the school's playing field. Seems it was a controversial decision at the time, but I think the inhabitants are generally happy with the benefits it's brought to the local community." The jury may still be out on the potential side effects of towers emitting invisible waves, I thought to myself, but the internet had improved many aspects of modern life. "Future generations may have webbed feet but -"

"Well, at least with a book shop game thing we are giving back a little, I suppose," Mum mumbled into her glass of merlot. It was heartening to see how my mother was slowly coming to terms with the prospect of her daughters taking on the Smith inheritance, though she was keen to change the subject. "This beef is rather good. Another perk of being back here in the country I guess, it was probably still mooing the other day."

"What an unpleasant thought!" Rosie continued to outline her plans. "Actually, I was thinking of cashing in on the Island's history as being a bit of a hippy haven. You know, have lots of vegan and vegetarian options. Maybe even be exclusively vegan? It's very on-trend right now. If we are going to bring Wesberrey kicking and screaming into the twenty-first century, then I think we should go the whole way. But at the same time, I want to keep that old book shop feel."

"It wouldn't need much in the way of interior design to do that. It's barely changed in a hundred years!" I joked. "Would you change the name? Island Books is not very original."

"Maybe we could do an homage to 'Friends' and call it 'Central Perk'?"

"Or not," Mum added with a decisive placing down of the water jug. "What about naming it after your father? If it wasn't for his shenanigans, you wouldn't be having this conversation."

"I think this is about a fresh start, Mum." My mother's statement was true, but had a bitter sting to it. "Why not name it after your side of the family? 'Bailey's Books' has a nice ring to it."

"Hmm, or 'Bailey's Book and Coffee Emporium'." Rosie sat back in her chair and sighed. "Sounds very Harry Potter-ish."

"But it doesn't sound like a place for gamers. We need something edgier." Luke pushed back his chair. Throwing a wary eye over to my mother, he asked: "May I leave the table to get a notepad and pen, please?" Mum acquiesced with a tilt of her head, and soon my nephew was playing with words and letters in between mouthfuls of beef and ale pie.

"Rosie, perhaps Zuzu can be a consultant on the vegan-vegetarian thing. She is a flexitarian or pescatarian or something." Mum waved her hands dismissively as she spoke. "I can't keep track, to be honest. It won't surprise you to know that Cindy has lots of those hippy friends you want to attract, so discuss it with her. I'm sure she will have lots of marvellous ideas." Pushing a morsel of burnt pie crust to the side of her plate, Mum turned her attention to me. "Have you had any more visions? Pam and Cindy are happy to get together tomorrow night if you have space in your hectic social schedule?"

"Mum, I have a job you know. And we are heading towards arguably the busiest week in my work calendar."

"Ah, yes, Easter, or actually the pagan festival of Eostre." Mum said rather pointedly. "Should I get in some chocolate eggs, then?"

Wanting to diffuse my mother's venom, which I knew was her defensive response to all this talk about the book shop, I replied, "Actually, I prefer the Lindt bunnies. Fill the house and garden with them as long as you don't go overboard on the Cadbury's Creme eggs. They are an abomination!"

"What about 'Dungeons and Vegans'? For the shop."

We all looked at Luke. Then looked at each other. 'Dungeons and Vegans' it is then.

Promises, Promises

Monday brought with it a soft rain and an unexpected visitor at the breakfast table.

"Barbara? I thought we agreed when I called around yesterday that you have to rest."

"Yes, Reverend Ward, we did, but I've spent most of the past week lying down on a bed and I am bored out of my mind. There is still so much to sort out for Palm Sunday, Easter and let's not forget the 'Walkathon'. It is still going ahead? Isn't it?"

"I don't know, Barbara. Most of the participants are still out of action, and we need to be respectful to Professor Linden and her family,"

"If you don't mind me saying so, Reverend. That is complete tripe. Helen Linden had no family to speak of. Her life was walking and being the 'Walkathon Champion' for seven years straight was her proudest achievement."

A prouder achievement than receiving a doctorate and gaining professorship, I wondered. It was a glorified sponsored walk, but hey, who am I to judge? Barbara was most insistent.

"I can't think of a better way to honour her memory, and I think you should reconsider. It's a major part of the Easter tradition here now and generates a lot of tourism."

"Well, let's discuss it later when we meet properly. Right now it seems there's an omelette being served on that plate with your name on it."

Cheese and mushroom omelette, no less, with a side order of grilled tomatoes. Mum loved to cook for guests more than she loved to provide for her family, and that meant she performed such catering activities with an abundance of love. Love that you could taste in every mouthful.

"Mum, how do you make these omelettes, seriously? I have tried time and time again to emulate your culinary prowess. I've watched and studied how you manoeuvre the mix in the pan to get an even coverage. I have marvelled at your folding technique, but my omelettes don't come close to your masterpieces. You should offer these in Rosie's cafe."

"I thought it was a *vegan* restaurant! Anyway, I'm not sure I am staying yet. I said I would think about it. I need to sell my house on the mainland, and as you well know, that is not shifting. The market is slow. One thing I do know is that if I return to Wesberrey permanently, it will be to retire. I want to spend time with my family as a gentle lady of leisure, not putting in a fifteen-hour day in a hot kitchen."

And certainly not in the kitchen of what was formerly your husband's mistress's shop. I understood. There was no point in pushing this subject any further.

"These are gorgeous though" Barbara raised her fork, put the last mouthful of the fluffy golden egg mix into her mouth, chewed briefly and swallowed loudly. "Needs a delicious cup of tea to finish it off. You stay seated, Beverley, I'll put the kettle on." Using the thumb and forefinger of her right hand to wipe away any stray crumbs, Barbara tried to get up, but Mum was having none of it. She leapt up and made a dramatic grab for the kettle. Barbara obediently settled herself back down at the table. "So, Rosie, you are opening a cafe? Sounds lovely. I don't suppose you have need of a local cake maker-extraordinaire?"

"Barbara, are you offering to sell me some of your amazing creations? Vegan, of course. That would be great." Rosie was keen to support Mum's point that eggs would be off the menu. "I'm no baker. I can manage a simple toasted sandwich or baked potato. I don't think it takes years at catering college to learn how to add a few sprigs of rocket and some sliced cherry tomatoes on the side and call it a salad garnish!"

"So, where are you thinking of opening the cafe?"

"Right here, in the old book shop."

Barbara's face and mood dropped. "What, on Market Square? The Smith's old place?"

"Yes, I am thinking of taking over the shop and Violet's old cottage."

"Oh yes. I forgot for a moment that she left everything to all of you. Erm, so just cakes and sandwiches?"

I realised that Barbara was working out in her head if this new venture would be competition for Phil's lunchtime trade in the pub. This required a timely intervention to ease her troubled mind.

"I think there is room for a tiny cafe serving fancy coffee and meat-free sandwiches. People who want a drink or a full meal will still use the 'Cat and Fiddle'. I think the chief trade will be in the morning when the pub is closed."

"There'll also be a gaming area at the back," chimed in Luke, who was keen to pick up the keys later that morning from Ernest so he could map out his plans. "It will be lit!"

"Ah, computer games, etc. So a place for youngsters to use words like 'lit'." Barbara laughed. "You won't be targeting Phil's silver-haired diners then. Not a place for the Rotary Club to hang out."

"Or the 'Wesberrey Walkers' on a late Saturday morning." Rosie pointedly nodded to me to back her up.

"No, not the 'Walkers'!" I shook my head in agreement. "But it will be a delightful spot to grab a coffee and read a book on market day. We must ensure the gaming room is sound-proofed, though."

"Bet." Luke shoved a piece of Marmite-coated toast in his mouth. Marmite, a yeast-based spread like Vegemite, and in my humble opinion disgusting, has a bitter tar-like consistency which turns my stomach. Luke is the only one in the house that goes anywhere near it. "We wouldn't want our gameplay interrupted by whichever Mr Darcy is better. Colin Firth, or what's his name."

"Matthew Macfadyen." Rosie seemed to drift off into a dreamlike state.

"You prefer the Keira Knightley Darcy? Really? Not Colin Firth striding across the estate with his wet shirt." I drifted off slightly myself.

"That bit is not in the book!"

"It's called artistic license, like Keira Knightley chasing chickens around. That's not in the book, either. Not sure Jane Austen would approve of her heroine getting covered in mud."

"They probably did, though. Especially on a rural estate like the Bennett's, Elizabeth famously arrived at Netherfield having walked for miles across country. She was a rebel. That's why Darcy loved her. Though he was both repulsed and attracted by her low-born ways, not least her muddy skirts and rosy glow."

"Girls! Enough. Rosie, you can discuss the societal nuances of 'Pride and Prejudice' to your heart's content when you open the book shop. Right now I suggest that you don't keep Mr Woodward waiting, and Jess, if you are so busy this week, you had better get a move on too."

Mum was obviously feeling the pressure. It must be hard on her. I think she wanted the kitchen back to herself for a while. One could always tell when she felt that a conversation had reached its natural conclusion. I wanted her to stay on Wesberrey so much. We were now complete. I knew she wanted that too and would eventually accept the changes that were to come. The selling of the house was a formality, but until it went through, she could still offer it up as a plausible alternative scenario. An escape, if she needed it.

"Mum, you could always rent your house out. It would give you a nice little income in your retirement," I offered.

"Hmm?" She replied like she hadn't considered that already, which knowing my mother she most definitely had. "Then I wouldn't have to work as a skivvy for my baby daughter. I'll think about it."

***

Taking our cue to leave my mother to tidy up the kitchen in peace, Barbara and I retired to my office to discuss what tasks remained to prepare for Palm Sunday later in the week.

"Palms ready for the blessing?"

Barbara opened a cardboard box she had only seconds before wrangled out of a cupboard at the opposite end of the room. "Check. There's plenty. Might need to reorder for next year, though."

"Excellent, and the readings? Do we have the actors cast? Who's playing Pilate?"

"Phil. He does it every year, and I have my one line as Pilate's wife." I noticed a wistful smile tweak the corner of her mouth. I needed to put a rocket under Phil the next time I saw him. They had to be together. *Just like Elizabeth and Darcy.* "You're the narrator. Tom loves to play Jesus, though he is getting a little too old to carry it off. He has a long curly wig he rolls out every year."

"Hmm, that will be something to look forward to. I hope no one else is dressing up."

"Gracious, no, just the wig. Ernest dies of embarrassment every year."

"I imagine he does. Well, I can see no point in messing with tradition, for now. Let's keep everything as it is and maybe we can look to getting some younger members of the parish involved next year. Jesus should be in his thirties. It's harder to appreciate the significance of his suffering when he's played by an octogenarian."

"Well, good luck with that one, Reverend. Anyway, I think we're all set. Can you get me up to speed on what the PCC talked about on Tuesday?" Barbara closed the box of palm crosses and sat on the chair opposite my desk with her trusty notebook in hand.

"Well, we discussed the 'Walkathon', obviously, but Helen Linden's memory aside, I'm still not sure it's wise to go ahead whilst there's potentially a poisoner on the loose." The naughty imp on my left shoulder urged me to take this moment to tease Barbara about God punishing sugar addicts during Lent, especially as she had failed, so far, to admit that she had broken her Lenten vow. The good angel on my right shoulder made me think better of it. A woman was dead. We needed to be serious. "What if the target of their attack was the 'Walkathon' or those associated with it? They might strike again!"

"Don't be silly, Judith didn't mean to give us all the runs as part of some grand plan to sabotage the race!" Barbara realised she had made a little pun and was quietly pleased with herself. "It was an accident. I think we should show our solidarity. She must be so upset about everything."

"I'm not so sure it was accidental, or that it was Judith. Did you know that her husband was having an affair?"

"What? Keith? I've known him for years. I mean, he's a nice man, but he's hardly Brad Pitt. Keith's just so... vanilla. I'm surprised he convinced Judith to sleep with him, let alone anyone else." Barbara found the whole notion of Keith the lothario very amusing. "Are you sure, Reverend? Who with? Anyone I know?"

Barbara scooted her chair closer to the desk. I had piqued her curiosity. Leaning across the two-foot mahogany void, I whispered, "Her cousin, Maureen!"

"Well, strip me down and call me Elvis! No way! Metal Maureen?"

"Metal Maureen?"

"Yes, they were in the same year as me at the Comp."

Oysterhaven Comprehensive (once Oysterhaven Technical College and now Oysterhaven Academy) was a large co-educational secondary school that took all local children over eleven who didn't secure a place at either of the single-sex grammar schools. It had a reputation for being a bit rough, and the numerous name changes hadn't changed that perception. Sam and I had gone to St. Mildred's Grammar School for Girls. Back in the day. Grammar kids and Comp kids didn't mix back then. I doubt if they do now. They were all several years younger than me, older children rarely socialise with the lower years. Thinking logically, they were probably all still in their respective primary schools when I left. As a result, all this local insight was new to me. I encouraged Barbara to carry on.

"They were both so skinny, all bones and sharp angles. So we called them 'Judy Joints' and 'Metal Maureen'. Kids can be so cruel. Hope not to offend, Vicar, but the boys used to joke about wearing protective clothing to have sex with them."

Despite warning me about the possible offence, I admit I was still shocked. It probably showed on my face because Barbara's tone immediately changed.

"Though, rumour has it that didn't stop them, the boys that is, from getting up to no good with the Sykes cousins. They had a bit of a reputation. I doubt it was fair. You know what teenage boys are like and how things spread."

Sadly, I did. The world still maintained these ridiculous double standards. What's good for the gander is still not equally good for the goose.

"Though the cousins were very competitive. Maureen was always copying Judith. Her hair, her clothes. But stealing her husband? I can't see it. Not after all these years."

"So, how did Judith end up with Keith? As you say, he's not the best looking of guys, though he seems a kind man. Protective and caring. Maybe that was the attraction?" I mentally chastised myself for being so shallow. Looks aren't everything.

"I heard that the attraction was that his family had the grocer's shop on Wesberrey. Rumour had it that Judith needed to get away from home. They married very young. I don't think she was even eighteen. If I remember right, people said it was a shotgun wedding. But they don't have any children, so maybe that was just more malicious gossip. Maureen never married. She's had several short-term relationships, but nothing stuck."

"Do you think Maureen was jealous of Judith, then?" I couldn't imagine the cousins I had witnessed talking so carefree, after the meeting in the vestry hall, being bitter love rivals. "This is crazy. We don't even know if Keith was having an affair with Maureen. Or that gave any of them a motive to poison the rhubarb jam. Enough tittle-tattle, we have a lot of work to do." I shuffled the papers in front of me.

Barbara stayed still in her chair, though her head tilted like the puppy on the logo of 'His Master's Voice'. Her eyes were wide with apprehension and her words uneasy. "So, Reverend. I guess you've figured out that I broke my vow. I have a very sweet tooth and I gave in to temptation. I am so ashamed."

"Barbara, please, it's not a cardinal sin, you know? You don't sign Lenten promises in blood. You haven't made a pact with the devil."

"I know, Reverend." Her face remained troubled. "But maybe if I had mentioned the jam treat earlier, they could have saved poor Helen! I should have admitted my sin straight away. I was blaming the dips when I knew it was probably the jam. I never eat hummus or salad."

I felt bad for my impish thoughts earlier. "You weren't to blame. Or alone. Avril blamed it on her gluten thingy. It still would have taken a while to narrow it down to the jam."

"Aargh! Oh, what a tangled web we weave, when first we practise to deceive."

Now she was quoting Sir Walter Scott. I took that as a cue to change the subject.

"Right, well, do we have enough Easter eggs for Sunday School?"

Lonely as a cloud

I convinced Barbara to return home and take the afternoon off. Rosie and Luke were off to view their new business venture, and as I thought Mum could do with some time alone, I offered to take the cat food up to the graveyard. To be honest, after all the drama of the past few days, I welcomed the chance to have some downtime myself. So, I set off to find a quiet spot with only the neighbourhood cats for company. Armed with the protective power of antihistamine tablets and the offer of food, I positioned myself on a small waterproof picnic sheet beneath the giant oak and waited for my feline friends to gather.

After the earlier shower, the afternoon sun was finally stepping up to warm the cold stones that surrounded me. A panorama of bright colours painted the scene. Fresh green grass, a screen of clear blue and the tiniest wisps of white floating across my eye line. Nature's bright hues a stark contrast to the grey stones catching the tiniest hint of yellow. Few families bury their loved ones in this graveyard anymore. Most of the headstones sat crookedly at the end of mossy and weed-covered plots. Some faded plastic flowers remained amongst the brown twigs of former bouquets. Amongst all the death and decay, an army of daffodils fought for survival. I hadn't really noticed them before. There was no wind that day. Though many had lost their heads in the previous storm, they still stood tall to support their comrades who had weathered it.

Life is beautiful.

We soldier on through grief and loss.

I rested my back against an old oak that had yet to sprout its leafy canopy and closed my eyes. I could sense that I was not alone. The odd tail brushed against me on its way to enjoy a late lunch, and the afternoon sun found my face and warmed me. There was nothing to fear, apart from the genuine risk of being disturbed by a passer-by, curious about the mad priest meditating under an ancient oak, surrounded by cats.

Fortunately, I was left alone. Tonight, I would gather two generations of sisters together to help me connect with my 'gift' — if I had one. One vision does not a medium make. I thought about how my mother had hidden this past from us. As a child, I wasn't aware of this side of my family's history even before we left the island. This was troubling, especially as I now knew that my mother practised with her sisters and, presumably, with her mother and aunts before that. Was the issue my father? My aunt Cindy said he put my mother on a pedestal, yet he was a serial adulterer. According to my older sister, rumours were rife across the island and she was aware of many rows where my mother always took him back. Even on the day of his death, which we now know was suicide, Mum was chasing after him. Was my father a narcissistic bully?

I had worked in several women's refuges and seen that it wasn't only physical violence they were fleeing. The gaslighting, the mind games, the ostracism from family and friends. That would explain a lot. It would also explain why neither I nor my sisters, missed his presence in our lives. We had instinctively stood by our mother, as tall and as strong as the daffodils around my feet.

***

Zuzu had reluctantly returned to join us for the evening meal at Pamela's house. Mum had made it very clear that this was important. Looking across the teak dining table in my aunt's back room at my sister's sullen face, I honestly hoped this gathering would live up to the hype.

Luke had opted to stay at the vicarage to look after Hugo. A weak excuse, but an understandable one. Another night of model railway talk offered little promise of fun to a modern teenage boy. We left him with instructions on how to reheat Mum's lasagne in the microwave, along with a cling-filmed bowl of salad to accompany it. I suspected that the bowl would still be untouched in the fridge when we returned. Luke's mission was to design a logo and theme for the new cafe's website. He had more than enough to keep him occupied whilst we were away.

The rest of the lasagne was now sitting in pride of place on an embroidered runner that cut the G-Plan table in two. Pamela's decor was not what one would expect from a witch or a wise woman. There were no herbs hanging from the ceiling joists and no dream catchers or wind chimes catching the breeze. That hippy chic was Cindy's territory. No, Pamela's house was floral and beige with the odd picture of the 'Flying Scotsman' or the 'Mallard' being the only nod that my uncle Byron lived there too.

Zuzu's sulky mood dominated the chat over dinner. Only Cindy was brave enough to move the conversation to the 'Baron'.

"Darling, how is the Inspector? Terrible thing, this poisoning. Rhubarb leaves, I understand. Very unfortunate."

"Dave is returning to duty tomorrow. They have brought him in to investigate that professor's death."

I wondered what there was to investigate? We know the source of the poison was the rhubarb jam.

"But surely that's a pretty cut and dried case. It was Judith's jam. He needs to interview the Hudsons. I have heard that Keith was having an affair with his wife's cousin." I decided it was time to put my theory out there to test the psychic knowledge in the room. "My gut is telling me it wasn't an accident. I think one of them planned to poison Maureen."

Pamela choked. "Well, we all know they are having an affair! That's hardly news!"

"Well, Barbara was shocked when I told her," I responded. "It can't have been that common knowledge."

"Barbara Graham sees nothing and knows everything." Pam washed down the remaining contents of her mouth with a swig of wine, took a breath and continued, "Don't misunderstand me, she's a treasure. One of those natural innocents we should cherish. Barbara always looks for the best in people and rarely sees any wrongdoing. Oh, she can gossip along with the best of us, but she sees people with a bit of a halo around them. Don't you agree, Cindy?"

"What? Barbara Graham? Oh, Pam, totally. She has a beautiful child-like aura. It's what we all love about her. She's always been on the outside of that friendship circle." Cindy waved her right hand in a vague circle over her plate. "You know, the Hudsons and the Matthews. They were a pretty wild bunch when they were younger. Funny how we turn out as we get older. We all settle, don't we? But I will be honest with you, I thought Keith's fling with Maureen ended years ago. Dear Maureen left on the shelf, and Judith all loved up. Maybe the poor darling just wouldn't let it go."

I had to know more. "Do you think Judith knows?"

"Well, she knew the first time around. Do you remember, Pam, she cut off all of Maureen's hair?"

"Oh my, yes. Both the Sykes girls had beautiful blonde locks. Rumour has it they had agreed to never get it cut. They were so close, they shared everything. Then Judith got married and came to live here. Oh, it must have been, what, five years or so later? Judith found out that Maureen had been sleeping with Keith all along. So she dragged her into the centre of Market Square, took a pair of garden shears and cut off Maureen's hair at the base of her ponytail!"

I was speechless!

Fortunately, Rosie leapt in with further questions. I just sat there enthralled by the tale that unfolded. With her blonde tail cast on the street before her, Maureen turned to her cousin and begged for forgiveness. She fell to her knees and raised her face, inviting whatever further punishment was in store. Judith knelt down where she stood, pulled her own ponytail around and taking the shears up to her shoulder, she lay her hair between its blades and cut. The two tails lay between them, on the cobbled street, in the shape of a heart.

"Keith stepped forward and took the shears from his wife. She didn't even flinch. They just knelt there. Looking at each other, eyes locked. It was several minutes before Stan and Audrey wrapped them both in their coats and coaxed them towards the 'Cat and Fiddle'." Pam slid her knife and fork across her now empty plate. "Anyone fancy a dessert? I have a cheesecake in the fridge, shop-bought I'm afraid but from their 'finest' range. Madagascan vanilla with frosted berries."

Whilst Pamela and my mother sliced up servings in the kitchen, Cindy continued the tale. "So, the cousins were as close as ever. They went to the salon together the next day and created for themselves a fresh look. The short-haired bob they sport today has been like a sign of kinship ever since. Oh, don't get me wrong, they remained über-competitive about everything. Take the 'Walkathon', for example. Every year they will both go to extraordinary lengths to beat each other. It's like watching an episode of that cartoon. The one with the dog and the purple villain... Dick Dastardly!"

"You mean 'Wacky Races'? But they always lose!" I was starting to wonder if there was any activity on Wesberrey that didn't hold scandal and intrigue.

"Yes, Darling and so did they. Every year, to Helen Linden."

"Aunt, you aren't suggesting they deliberately tried to nobble the opposition?"

Pamela and Mum had rejoined us at this point. There was a beat before Cindy answered my question and when she did, both her sisters joined her in creepy unison.

"Don't be silly, dear. Someone else killed Helen Linden."

***

I had learnt to trust their intuition. They were right before. If only I could access their insight. Though it appeared to be more of a *knowing* rather than actual knowledge. They were certain they *knew* what they knew but were annoyingly short on any facts or evidence that might help solve the case.

Regardless of this vagueness, I wanted to push myself. Whilst I still wasn't convinced I shared this family gift, or subscribed to all that came with it, I was excited to see what plans my aunts had to help me to a greater connection.

After dessert, all six of us went upstairs. Pamela's unprepossessing house had three bedrooms on the first floor. One was for her and Byron, and the other was their son's old bedroom. Both faced the front of the house. Also on this floor was an airing cupboard which housed an immersion boiler and another door led to the bathroom. It was the fifth door off the small landing at the back that led to the most intriguing part of the house. A place that few visitors would ever see. Her 'spell' room.

Inside there was no furniture except for a workstation in the centre. The wooden island was topped with a slab of solid black marble, much like you would find in an upmarket kitchen and in the plinth beneath were cubby holes filled with wicker baskets you could access from either side. There was one narrow window on the back wall, covered by a blackout curtain. The only light came from candles safely held in a myriad of clear hurricane jars. These jars hung from the ceiling and sat on the various shelves that lined the walls alongside other small jars containing a variety of herbs and other spell paraphernalia. On the marble worktop stood a single-ringed portable gas stove - an unattractive green puce, which slightly ruined the aesthetic.

My aunt mistook my screwed-up face as concern for my health and safety. "Don't worry, darling. We aren't doing any fire work today." Cindy took the portable stove off of the counter and placed it on a shelf behind her. "Let's hold hands."

My sisters and I jostled for position around the island. None of us spoke.

"Now," said Cindy, "I need you all to focus on your breathing. Listen to my words and do exactly as I say. Do not break the chain until I tell you to. Do not open your eyes, unless I tell you to. And open yourself up to the possibilities. Try not to question or judge. Just allow. Do we understand?"

We nodded.

"Jess, darling, you want to explore your gift of second sight. You want us to help you open up your third eye. To help you harness your sixth sense." I tried not to laugh at the numerically-based litany. I had to take this seriously. All of us were here because of me. I was sure I could feel my mother's disapproving eyes burning into me, which was crazy because I know we all had our eyes closed. Or did we? Perhaps I should take a sneaky peek. Yes, we were, well all except for me. I immediately squeezed my eyes shut again.

Cindy instructed us to breathe deeply, to bring in love, and exhale any tension. A stillness enveloped the room. Our breathing ebbed and flowed in a syncopated rhythm of gentle inhalations and louder, more forceful outward breaths. Maybe it was the increase in carbon monoxide or the heat from six warm bodies, but I felt a little light-headed. Cindy's instructions called through the fog in my mind.

"I want you to imagine there is a ball of light at your feet. The ball is swirling around your toes and ankles looking for an invitation. Invite it in. Call it up. See it fill and expand through your legs. It fills your stomach and your chest. You can feel its energy exploring your entire body. It reaches down to your fingertips and up through your throat. It illuminates your breaths. You are one with the light. You breathe it in and breathe it out. It is your inner fire. Your life force. It connects you to all that is. Embrace it. Allow it to flow within you and through you. Now, everyone, turn towards Jess. Focus on her. Jess, in your mind, see the love. Darling, I want you to feel the warmth of our attention. Open your mind and your heart. Receive us. We are here as one, together. We sisters three. The power of two generations. We stand together. Welcome us in."

My head spun. An electric blue light cocooned me. I felt scared and secure in equal measure. I was breathing; I knew I was breathing, I could feel my chest rising up and down and yet, I felt paralysed. Whatever was happening had suspended all of my normal body rhythms. I could feel the floor beneath my feet, yet it seemed as if I was floating. I wanted to let go, to travel through time. Part of me knew that I could. Part of me held on tighter. Firmer. To lose my grip would send me spiralling away from those I loved. From my home. From my anchor in this universe.

Mum's voice reached out to pull me back in. "Jessie? Jess? You can come back now. We are still here. We are waiting for you."

***

"You went white!"

"Yes, like a ghost! It was eerie. You were totally zoned out!"

"What did it feel like? Were you like astral planing or something? You definitely left us for a while, little Sis."

"I don't know. It was so quick."

"Quick? You were like that for a good half hour. Zuzu and I were getting worried, but the 'sisterhood' over there were as calm as you like. Freaked the life out of me, I can tell you. Not sure I want to do that again in a hurry. But it was fun."

Rosie was cuddling up to me on Pamela's floral sofa. I must have been in a trance. All that carbon monoxide and too much cheesecake. But half an hour? I was sure it was only a few moments.

"Did you see anything? Crack the case? Can I tell Dave to take the day off and get back into bed?"

I looked at both my sisters, their eyes eager for some insights but, as the seconds slipped by, my memory of what I had seen, or rather not seen but sensed, weakened. "I felt like I was... I don't know how to describe it, removed?" I glanced through the alcove that linked Pamela's living and dining rooms. The 'sisterhood' was deep in conversation. "What did you guys feel?"

"Empowered," answered Rosie. We both looked at Zuzu.

"Er, I felt... liberated. Free. Can you actually believe we just did that? Whatever it is, we just did."

"The question is," Rosie sat up and took my hand and reached across for Zuzu's. "Could we do it again, by ourselves, I mean."

"What? Without Cindy?" I wasn't sure I would want to do whatever it was we just did.

"Or Pamela, or Mum. If you are the next 'godmother' then we should be able to. And Zuzu, what about your daughters: Clara, Phoebe, and Freya - isn't she next in line? I really think you should tell them about tonight."

"Hold on, I don't think we need to be too hasty." I straightened myself up. This was a serious conversation. I was having a difficult enough time coming to terms with this 'gift', such as it was. I wasn't ready to contemplate it becoming Freya's inheritance, too.

"Jessie, our little sister is right. I have to tell them. They have a right to know and to be honest, I wish we had. Earlier, I mean. Imagine our lives if we knew we had this ability inside us."

I couldn't. I wanted to embrace this knowledge, I really did. There was no denying now that it was real, and at that moment, it felt like the most natural thing in the world. But how would this fit into the actual world outside our family bubble? The world in which I was a vicar in the Church of England.

The one thing I did know was that my mother and aunts were right. I *knew* that someone else had poisoned Helen Linden. The hazy bit was who?

Torn

Tuesday morning landed with a bump. I had to run some errands before the business part of my day started, so I had planned to jump on 'Cilla' the moment the sun threw her first rays over the horizon and head straight to Market Square. I wanted to catch Keith and Judith before they set up their stall. Whilst I psychically knew that neither of them was responsible for Helen Linden's death, there were still a few loose ends to tie up. Did both or either of them deliberately set out to poison anyone? Was it to get at Maureen and everyone else affected were collateral damage, so to speak? Or was their intention to nobble the other walkers to improve Judith's, or Wesberrey's chances at the title this year?

I am not naturally an early riser; it is a weary routine borne from the necessity of life. If the world left me to lie in all morning, most days I probably would. To add injury to insult, occasionally my ageing body surprises me with a random twinge or some obscure pain apparently caused merely by the act of sleeping. My body plotting with my mind to make me fall straight back down on my mattress and stay there forever.

Today was one of those days, probably something to do with last night's exertions. Today's twisted limb of choice - my neck! The best medicine was to soldier on. At least I didn't have to walk too far, thanks to 'Cilla'. The weight of the cycle helmet, though, was not helping. By the time I got to Market Square, the dull ache in my shoulders had developed into a stiff crick. My head was struggling to stay upright. Not an impressive look for interrogating suspects. It's difficult to come across as menacing with your head tilted to the side at a jaunty angle.

Keith appeared to be setting up the stall alone.

"Morning, Keith! How is Judith doing? I was hoping to catch her, check everything is alright."

"Thank you for asking, Reverend. Judith is staying home for a few days. She spent all of yesterday cleaning the kitchen. Steam cleaning every surface. Disinfectant everywhere. The smell is overpowering. To be honest with you, I am relieved to be out here in the fresh air."

"No 'Hudson's Homemade' today? I suppose that is wise. I remember you mentioned changing the branding after mass on Sunday. That's an inspired idea. Once all this furore dies down. Are you covering Maureen's stall as well then?"

"Well, seems the least I can do, in the circumstances." Keith was unpacking boxes of produce from a small Piaggio Ape van. Most of the traders used these or horse-drawn carts to transport their wares across the island. I recalled that Judith had used a quad bike. It's a godsend the roads of Wesberrey are in such excellent condition, or none of those jars would have made it back in one piece. Keith cut off my musings by dropping a heavy box of root vegetables on the stand. "Is there anything, in particular, I can help you with this morning, Reverend? It's just I am on my own, and it will get really busy soon."

"Sorry, of course." This was my moment. I straightened my neck and cut to the point. "Keith, did you poison the rhubarb jam?"

My abruptness took him aback. He collapsed into the folding chair behind the stall in a slump.

The sudden force of his weight caused the metal legs of the chair to buckle slightly.

"How did you know?"

Wow, that was a stroke of luck! One direct question, and I almost have a confession.

"To be honest, I didn't until right now. Do you want to tell me why?"

"Aw, Reverend. It will be a relief to talk to someone. I don't know what got into me. You would think me the luckiest man in the world. It's every fella's dream, isn't it? Two beautiful women. But it's exhausting!"

Oh my, what was I supposed to do now? Pretend I didn't know what he was talking about. Act shocked? Well, that bit was easy.

"So, you were having an affair, and you thought to get yourself out of this mess you would kill your lover off? Who was your intended victim? Because you took down several beautiful women."

"Maureen, of course. Oh, Reverend, I know you must've heard the rumours. Nothing stays a secret for long in this place."

This was true, everyone knew it seems, except for my parish secretary.

"Well, yes. I had heard a few things. But the cousins seem to have such a close bond. Why would Maureen want to do this? Why would you? And why use Judith's jam? What did you hope to achieve?" The direct questions poured out. Keith sat soaking them up like a heavy-duty sponge cloth.

"They confused me. Sometimes I would call out the other's name when we were, you know, in the throes of passion. They didn't seem to mind, though. It was a game to them, and I was their plaything." Keith threw his hands up and used his fingers to raise and sift his salt 'n' pepper hair. "I suppose I had had enough. Reverend Ward, I am more than just a sex toy. I'm a normal man. A dutiful husband. I just tried to keep everyone happy. They are insatiable! I wanted to send them both a message. I was at the end of my tether, but I honestly didn't want anyone else to get hurt."

Keith crumpled in the creaking chair. I felt he would have freely cried if he had any tears left. He had spent them already. A long time ago, I suspected. This desperate act was years in the making.

120

"So, Keith. Help me understand. You used Maureen's rhubarb to poison Judith's jam. Killing two birds with one stone, so to speak." Part of me could appreciate the artistry of his plan. "But how did you do it? Did you add the rhubarb leaves to the jam during the canning process? Judith said that she let no one in the area whilst she was cooking."

"And she doesn't." Keith adjusted his frame in the chair. Its steel feet scraped the cobbles beneath. "I batched up the jars for the meeting at the vicarage, so it was easy for me to reopen them. I stirred in the ground leaves and then resealed the jars. It didn't take long."

"How do you do that? The resealing bit. Is that even possible?" My knowledge of the art of fruit preservation was woefully inadequate for this interrogation.

"We often reseal the jars that fail during the canning process. It's a chore that Judith often leaves to me. I quality check all batches, so there was no reason for her to suspect any foul play. It's a very simple process."

Like any good comic villain, Keith seemed keen to explain his plan. The more he opened up the more I sensed an element of pride in his elaborate scheme.

"All you have to do is place fresh lids on jars, screw on the rings and lower them back into the pot. Boil for ten minutes. Then rest, it takes about twelve hours. They make a lovely pinging sound as they seal." He smiled. "The labels come off in the boil, but that's a quick fix once they have cooled down."

"So it was just the rhubarb jam. You didn't put the ground leaves into anything else?"

"No. It's Maureen's favourite, but I wouldn't know which jar she would take, so I had to lace them all. I didn't expect it to be so popular. Nobody else ever takes the rhubarb, but I guess they thought they would try something new as there were no 'Bakewell Tart' ones. That's where my brilliant plan unravelled. I stupidly dropped the 'Bakewell' tray as we were loading the quad. I smashed the whole batch to smithereens!"

"Keith, you know I will have to tell PC Taylor about this."

He nodded.

"It's a fair cop. At least I'll get some rest in jail!"

Feeling Hot, Hot, Hot!

That evening's Walkers Workout saw the welcome return of Avril and Barbara to our ranks. News of Keith Hudson's arrest was naturally the primary topic of conversation. So enthralled was the group by the day's revelations that Frederico was struggling to get anyone's attention. He was in a fairly foul mood already, as he had still not heard anything about the position at Stourchester University. His frustration and anger were building with every missed star jump and box step.

"Ladies! Ladies! We have less than two weeks before the Walkathon. We have lost two of our finest walkers." I assumed he was referring to Judith and Keith. We all doubted Judith would rejoin the group anytime soon. "The rest of you are wasting my time! You have no ambition. Vocês são todos burros!"

"Hey! Did you just call us donkeys?" Having just gotten her sister back from the claws of death, Verity was in no mood for insults. "Avril, remember when we did that 'burros' tour of Paderne in the Algarve?"

"I do. It was stunning but so hot!" Avril's recent illness had not in any way affected her flirting ability as she made the most of the word 'hot' flicking a seductive eye towards Frederico and fanning her cleavage with a flat hand. Her new tank top was earning its keep reining in her heaving breasts.

"Stop that now! You're *still* flirting after he called you an ass?" Verity ripped the sweatband from her brow and threw it dramatically to the floor. Then she stomped on it with her neon pink trainers to emphasise her point. "I've had enough of this charade. We still aren't going to win this stupid walkathon. One of our group is sitting in a cold jail cell this evening whilst we all prance about as if nothing has happened. He tried to poison us all! Avril, I could have lost you! He killed that professor woman. I mean, I didn't like her, but no one deserves to die like that. Just so he could warn off Maureen bloody Sykes! Twisted and perverted!"

Frederico stood at the front of the hall, clapping his hands in a ridiculous attempt to regain order. I shot a look over to Barbara, who headed straight to the kitchen; she knew what we needed to calm the situation. Great minds think alike. I went to stand beside Frederico and gently pulled his hands down to stop the pointless clapping. I had to take charge.

"Walkers!" I called out in the shrillest voice I could muster to cut through the noise. "I think what we all need right now is a nice cup of tea. Barbara has already put on the kettle. Let's pull across some chairs and get ourselves comfortable."

The group obediently walked over to the chair stacks at the other end of the hall and soon we regrouped in a circle, much like the one we had sat in with our 'Walkathon' guests. Curiously, even though many of our party had not been at that meeting, we all instinctively left a chair vacant. The one on the spot where Helen Linden had sat just over a week ago.

"I'm sorry for my little outburst." Verity balanced her cup and saucer on her knee. "It's been so stressful. What with Avril at death's door and looking after the salon by myself. And then the news today. Poor Judith."

"And poor Maureen!" Audrey interjected. The school secretary obviously felt the need to defend her friend. "That bastard Keith tried to kill her, and then he sent her roses. Red roses! The gall of that man!"

"What Keith did was very wrong," I offered. "But I think he was desperate, torn between two demanding women. It's easy for us to judge when we don't know the full details."

"Well, you seem to know a lot about 'desperate' men for a member of the cloth, Vicar!" Audrey was on a roll. "And you're certainly in no position to judge." Looking around the group for support, she added, "We all know you are a bit of a vamp yourself!"

With all the drama of the past few days, and the not insignificant effect of the continuing neck pain on my general mood, I wasn't willing to turn the other cheek to this personal attack.

"Audrey, I want to say this is neither the time nor the place for this, but as you raised it." I straightened myself as upright in the chair as my neck would allow. "Let me be very clear. I have no designs on your husband. Stanley is very nice, but I am not interested in him or any other man."

I probably should have timed my response a little better — several group members were now choking on their beverages.

"The Reverend? After your Stan!" Barbara was the first to stop coughing. "Oh, Audrey, you are a wag! No one is after your man."

Audrey found a new victim for her vitriol. "Well, you only have eyes for the verger! Isn't it about time you acted on all that pent-up sexual desire, *Miss* Graham, eh?"

"Dat is quite enough, Mrs Matthews!" Martha put her teacup and saucer down on her lap with a level of authority that made us all sit up straighter. "No need to attack Ms Graham or Reverend Ward. Two nicer women yuh couldn't hope to find. If the Reverend prefers ladies, dat ain't none of our business."

"No, Martha, I didn't mean I was... Not that it would matter if I was, but... I just meant that I wasn't interested in getting involved with anyone right now." This conversation was taking a very unexpected turn.

It was Avril that brought us back to a topic we could all unite around.

"Ladies, and gentleman, I think we all deserve a special treat after all this nastiness." She reached out for her sister's hand across a sulking Frederico reluctantly sat between them. "Pop by the salon tomorrow morning and you can all have a free 'do', on us. Everyone's invited and I won't accept any excuses. We have some openings first thing, so Verity and I will see you all for wash 'n' blow-dry at nine-thirty sharp."

The twins looked at each other and smiled, united in their love of hair and beauty. The rest of us were relieved by the change of subject. The offer of free haircuts seemed to have restored the cosmic balance.

***

'Scissor Sisters' was buzzing when I arrived just a little after half-past nine. I am not a big fan of professional hairdressers, just like I am not much of a follower of fashion in any area. Family and friends have often been scathing in their assessments of my sartorial style. I trim my hair myself using a technique invented by British hairdresser, Lee Stafford. Basically, you brush all your hair to the front, gather it in a ponytail in the centre of your forehead on the hairline, pull the tail down to your desired shortest length and cut. You do a bit of snipping into the remaining end to create more gentle layers, and that's it. I haven't messed with my hair colour, mainly because I'm not that adventurous, though I really admire those that are brave enough to sport a vivid shade. My sister Zuzu is a natural blonde, and Rosie a stunning auburn, like my mother. I got the runt colour-mousy brown. Now with age, I have a few silvery-white highlights, and that's the most exciting it's ever been. I was secretly hoping that they would be too busy to get to me. Such hope was dashed the minute I walked through the door.

"Reverend! Over here! I have been reserving this chair just for you." Verity pulled out the black leather chair in front of her. As I approached, she snapped her fingers and an assistant, a teenage girl with an asymmetric peroxide blonde bob, shaved on the left side to reveal a layer of shocking pink, scurried over to ask me if I wanted anything to drink.

"A cup of tea would be lovely, I'm gasping!"

Verity guided me round to sit facing a large full-length gilt-edged mirror. A third of the way down there was a shelf cluttered with hairdressing paraphernalia. Verity magically produced a black plastic cape and flicked it in place around my body, tying it at my neck with the style and precision of a Spanish matador. Lifting my hair from the back she completed the look with a silicone neck shield.

"So, Vicar. Avril and I have been waiting for months to get our hands on you. Played a game of rock, paper, scissors over a glass of pink gin last night and I won! Avril is gutted. Look at her!"

Avril looked perfectly fine to me. She was engaged with Barbara's cropped blonde perm. They were deep in conversation. From the occasional lifting and stretching out of her client's wet hair, I think the conversation centred mainly around the desired length of the cut, but it could have been about UFOs or chocolate pudding. I couldn't hear a word above the thumping music coming out of the speakers mounted precariously above the sinks and the general hub-bub of the salon. I could barely hear Verity, and she was talking right by my ear.

Martha was sitting in the chair next to mine. A striking young man, with cheekbones 'to die for' and a flair for hair of African origin was showing her style examples from a large folder. Audrey was at the nail station. Remembering last night's bitter exchange, I tried not to catch her eye.

Despite the noise, it is customary, I believe, to engage in small talk at the hairdressers, so I kicked off first. "No Frederico then? That's a shame. I supposed he thinks this women-only area is off-limits."

"But we are unisex. It says it clearly on the sign out front. Though I understand, poor lamb. All the hormones in here this morning. He'd be lucky to get out alive!" Verity took the metal end of her comb and used it to lift sections of my hair. "Now, Reverend Ward. Is this the hair of a modern vicar? Or a crime-fighting super sleuth? I think not! You need something with more va va vroom! I mean, I'm all for keeping things 'au naturel' but your hair is undecided, isn't it? Is it brown? Is it grey? And, if you don't mind me saying so, you are still in your prime, Vicar. You've great skin. Let's make the most of those eyes, eh? A warm tone... I'm thinking of a 'Caramel Latte'."

"What to drink? No, I asked for tea. Don't want to be too much trouble!"

"No, for your hair. 'Caramel Latte', it's a shade. Dwayne, what do you think, sweetie? 'Caramel Latte' or a nice 'Chestnut'?" Dwayne swung my chair around and stood for a few moments, the forefinger of his right hand rubbing over his lips in deep contemplation.

"Hmm, well I think there's a hint of green in them brown wonders so I say 'Bright Toffee', give those warm tones a bit of magic!"

"Dwayne, you are a genius! Let me get the colour chart. Toffee is inspired. Vicar, you cannot refuse. On the house. The works. Not just the wash 'n' blow-dry. Dwayne, I'm thinking a smooth bob?"

"Honey, you read my mind! Martha, my love. I'll be right back. Verity and I have some cooking to do."

Left alone as our stylists went to the back room to mix up a bowl of 'Bright Toffee', Martha and I sat back with our cups of tea and relaxed.

"I guess there is no point in arguing?" I shrugged.

"Oh, not once Dwayne is fired up. He is a chemical wizard! And what dat boy can do with a 'fro? I told Avril last night, I would only come if he's on shift today. She said, 'Of course!' and here I am."

"Such a gracious thing for the twins to do, isn't it? After all we've been through."

"They are so sweet. And, yuh know, Audrey's okay too. I don't know why you two haven't hit it off better. She gets very protective of her Stan."

"I had noticed." I laughed.

"But now we know that yuh aren't into men like that she will back down."

"Martha, I *am* into men. Just not right now, and not Stan. *Never* Stan.."

"Doesn't matter to me either way, Vicar. We are all God's children. Just like that poor sweet Professor Linden. Plenty of rumours about her too, but no one should die of cyanide poisoning. What an awful way to go. Her last minutes on this earth would have been excruciating."

"What did you just say? Helen Linden died from cyanide poisoning, not oxalic acid?" I *knew* it wasn't the rhubarb jam!

"Yes, Dr Sam told me. They completed the autopsy yesterday afternoon."

I needed to have a chat with my best friend, just as soon as I could escape from Verity's clutches!

***

"So why didn't you tell me about the cyanide? Eh?" I had given Martha a lift back to the hospital, mainly because that is the neighbourly thing to do, and also because it gave me an excuse to hunt down her boss for more details on the cause of Profesor Linden's death.

"I like your hair by the way." Sam was avoiding the issue, though I will admit Verity had performed nothing short of a miracle with my toffee coloured bob.

"Don't change the subject. You know this means that someone deliberately set out to kill Helen Linden, don't you? I have to find out who."

"And that is exactly why I didn't tell you. You know, I believe that they have put a highly distinguished detective inspector on the case." Sam busied herself with some folders in the filing cabinet. "It's Dave's job, not yours. Find somebody to pray over or something." Sam turned to me and pushed her specs back up her nose, which was usually a sign that she was being serious. I could feel her exasperation at my wanting to dig deeper and knew it was borne out of a loving concern for my safety. It was sweet. "Jess, do you want a cup of tea, or maybe even something stronger? I still have a stash of alcoholic gifts from —"

"Grateful patients, I know. Funny how they never give you flowers or cake. Your reputation as a lush is obviously a truth universally acknowledged."

"Hmm, misquoting Austen at me now, eh? Do you want some tea or not?"

"Not. I am still swimming in the stuff from the salon."

I realised that I still knew very little about Helen Linden outside of her being pagan in her religious leanings, a leading expert on Mary Wollstonecraft and the athletic owner of a shapely rump. These were unlikely motives for murder. I wished that my 'gift' gave me more actual clues and fewer 'feelings'. Perhaps it would tune in better if I went to where Helen Linden lived or worked.

How would I get into her house? I don't even know where she lives!

I'll call Eunice. She must know. Anyway, I needed to talk to her about Helen's funeral. Reverend Cattermole was still in hospital, so that was the perfect pretence. Now the autopsy was complete, they would release the body to Leo Peasbody within days.

"Sam, I don't suppose you have heard anything about when they are releasing her body. I understand Leo is taking charge of the arrangements."

Sam's cheeks flushed a delicate pink. Leo would have an address. I tried to control the twitch at the corner of my mouth. I needed to play it very cool. Perhaps if I asked Sam politely, she would reach out to her booty partner and — she was way ahead of me.

"No. I am not calling him to get Helen Linden's address or any other details for you. I know you, Jessamy Ward. I'm all for solving a puzzle, but murder by cyanide poisoning! Someone extremely calculating and evil is behind this, and I don't want you anywhere near them. Do you understand? Leave it to the police!"

Down on the Farm

A timely phone call when I arrived back at the vicarage established that I would meet with Eunice at Maureen's farm shop at three o'clock the following day. Eunice had been working there part-time for the past few years and had stepped up to run things full-time whilst Maureen was in the hospital. Eunice was happy to chat once the shop was closed. They were short-staffed and she would be too busy to give me her full attention whilst the shop was open. That worked well for me. I decided to make the most of the trip to Oysterhaven and pop in to see Reverend Cattermole beforehand.

It was a relief to see Richard sitting up in bed and reading when I arrived. He was still pale and machines were monitoring his vitals, but he was brighter and in quite a chatty mood.

"Terrible business with Professor Linden. Not much of a church-goer, but still a lovely lady. We had many a long talk about the role of the traditional church in the systemic oppression of women. She was very excited about meeting you, Reverend Ward. Helen was a keen researcher on local female folklore and, of course, your family features a lot in those ancient tales. But then you would know more about all that than I do."

Ancient tales, local folklore? There was still a lot I had to learn about my family's past.

"Sadly, I know very little about my roots. It wasn't something we talked about when I was young. Now I am back on Wesberrey I should probably find out more."

"Well, if you want me to put you in touch with the local history society, just say the word. They have been begging to poke around inside your church for years. Eccentric bunch - but harmless. Helen would turn in her grave if you were to invite them to open up the Abbey Well."

There's a well in the church? The legend is of the Goddess of the Triple Wells, so I guess the one in Aunt Pamela's garden is one of three. If the second is in St. Bridget's, where is the third one?

Richard was on a roll. "She didn't put much stock in their amateur ways, though. Best leave it a while. Let her indignant spirit settle."

Or at the very least until she was in the grave she could turn in! As she'd been murdered, I think she would have every right to feel a bit resentful. Such dark commentary from a fellow member of the clergy, though, didn't feel very respectful. Not that I could judge. I desperately wanted to learn more about the Abbey Well. A conversation to bank for another time.

"Richard, do you have any idea who would want Helen Linden dead? Surely you aren't suggesting the local history society?"

"Oh, dear Lord, no! They are very much from the metal detectors brigade. I think they would lose sleep if they accidentally disturbed an ants' nest. It surprised me to hear that it was Keith Hudson who poisoned the jam, though. I have read enough Agatha Christie to know that poison is usually the weapon of choice for the female of the species."

"But Keith didn't kill Helen. She died from cyanide poisoning" At least this statement could now stand firm on actual evidence, not just my psychic hunch.

"Hmm, so maybe it was a woman after all? Curious there should be victims to two different poisoners at the same time." Richard popped a grape into his smug mouth. He was enjoying this.

"Well, not if the second poisoner took advantage of the misdirection offered by the first poison. The murderer would have needed to act swiftly to respond in time. Perhaps hoping that their wicked deed would remain hidden amongst the confusion of the others.

It suggests that this was something they had planned for a while and then enacted quickly to make the most of the opportunity."

Richard rubbed his bald head as if the friction of the movement would stimulate his 'little grey cells'. "Except... Helen didn't buy any of Judith's jam at the meeting. She only ever buys the 'Bakewell Tart' variety. My favourite too, as it happens. But I thought, well, it's good to try something new once in a while. Helen was most put out, as I recall. She could be extremely black and white like that. All or nothing."

"So, you are telling me she didn't buy any jam? Not a single jar?"

"Nope, not a one. So, thankfully, that eliminates anyone at the meeting, surely, as they would have known that."

"Well, I didn't spot it. I wonder if the police have found the murder weapon yet?"

I thought it might be an excellent time to check up on the Baron's health.

***

"Zuzu? It's just a teeny-tiny favour." I knew I couldn't go directly to the source, but my sister had a talent for persuasion. If Dave was going to let slip something pertaining to the case, Zuzu would be the one to get it for me. "Otherwise, I might have to break into the house and you wouldn't want me caught for trespassing, would you?"

"I can't believe that you are asking me to interfere with official police business!"

"I'm not. I'm merely asking you to put some feelers out. What did they find at the scene? Do they know how the killer administered the poison? You know, nothing major."

"Mum will kill me if she finds out I'm colluding with you. She warned you to stay away from this."

"Yes, and when did you ever do anything Mum told you to do? Don't start now!"

"Okay, I'll call him." I could hear the resignation in my sister's voice. "But you have to promise me you won't go anywhere near the professor's house. Just talk to that woman about her funeral. That's your job. Then straight home."

I promised.

Sitting astride 'Cilla', I punched the address of Maureen's farm shop into the GPS on my phone. The farm was at least a fifteen to twenty-minute drive away. I needed to get my skates on to catch Eunice as she was closing up. It would be rude to keep her waiting.

I was in such a hurry that I almost didn't notice a familiar car pulling up next to me at the corner junction. It was Conrad. I waved and he wound down his window.

"Where are you heading at this hour?" He asked.

"I'm going to see Eunice at the farm shop. We need to sort out the details for Helen's funeral."

"Ah, yes. She's spending a lot of time there at the moment. We all must do what we can for Maureen at this time. I'm driving that way myself. Need to jump in there quickly now that Keith is out of the way. Her farm backs onto my east field, you see. It would be a marriage made in heaven. Follow along behind, Jess, old girl. The farm can be a devil to find if you don't know the area."

Old girl! Letting that comment slide, I allowed Conrad to turn first out of the junction and pulled in behind. The country lanes around Oysterhaven all look the same, and the locals aren't very sympathetic to a vicar on a scooter trying to find her way. I was grateful for the escort.

I parked 'Cilla' in a space outside the shop and waved goodbye to Conrad. So, he knew about Keith, and Maureen too. It really was the world's worst kept secret. His car wheels spun in haste as he turned his attention to his ultimate quarry. Gravel from the tyres spluttered across the car park. Hopefully, this romantic development would mean his recent pursuit of me was also scattered in the dust. A farm offers a much bigger prize than a vicar.

The car park was empty except for one dusty cream Mini Clubman Estate I assumed must belong to Eunice. The farm was too remote to get here without your own transport. The exterior of the farm shop was unassuming. It looked like an old barn conversion. Outside stood two sacks of potatoes, a few more bags marked charcoal, and stacks of fire logs. An empty plant rack stood close to the door. Sprinklings of spent soil in varying circles were the only hints that pots had stood there earlier. Eunice must have already moved some merchandise back inside the store for security. That and the empty car park suggested that all the customers had left. We should be able to have a friendly conversation without fear of being disturbed.

I pushed through heavy wood doors to find a surprisingly bright interior. Fluorescent lights hung down from the rafters above, illuminating rows of polished wood shelves filled high with fresh produce of all kinds. There were plump collections of fruit and vegetables in every colour of the rainbow. Several refrigerated units had white trays holding the finest cuts of meat, each tray interlaced with plastic green parsley heads. Cupboards stored jars of herbs, dressings and other exotic condiments. This was a foodie's paradise. Under a sign mimicking gingham bunting stood rows of 'Hudson's Homemade' jams and preserves. I was obviously in the right place, but there was no sign of Eunice anywhere.

I called out.

I heard a muffled voice from a room at the back. Then a bang, accompanied by what sounded like glass bottles rolling around on concrete. A run of expletives cut through the awkward silence that followed until, finally, Eunice emerged at a door at the end of the food hall.

"Sorry about that, Reverend Ward. I knocked over the empties. We have a scheme for reusing milk bottles, you see. I collect them during the day, and one of the farmhands takes them up to the bottling plant in the morning."

Eunice appeared gaunt around the face, her hair straggly. Maybe it had just been a very busy day. It can't be easy running a place like this on your own, and she would be grieving her old friend too.

"Here, Eunice. Why don't you take the weight off your feet for a little, eh? Do you want me to put on the kettle? Just point me in the right direction, and then we can relax and talk through the arrangements for Helen's farewell service."

Eunice pointed vaguely toward some tables and chairs off to the side. As I moved closer, I saw there was a kitchen at the back with a small barista machine, a black cast iron potato oven, a microwave, and a tiny fridge. In front was a chiller containing white tubs of sandwich fillings.

"I need to put the lids on," Eunice commented as I peered to inspect the selection on offer. "Did you want a quick sandwich? It won't take long to knock one up."

"If it's not too much trouble, the tuna mayo looks good. On wholemeal, if that's okay? I'll make the drinks."

Once rested a little, Eunice appeared to brighten. There were obvious dark shadows under her eyes, and a general puffiness suggested that she had been crying a lot recently. When we had finished the sandwiches, she offered some cake.

"Oh, that sounds lovely. You sit down, I'll look. What do you fancy?" I moved closer to the clear glass cloches on the counter. "There's apple tart, one pretty tired looking slice of lemon meringue and, ooh, is this a Bakewell tart?" I could swear I saw Eunice flinch. I suppose it reminded her of Helen. Here I go again, putting my size five shoes in my mouth. "You must miss her a lot."

"Who?" Eunice looked at me, her puffy eyes ready to burst any second. The cake could wait. I returned from around the other side of the counter and sat back down beside her with a hastily grabbed paper serviette. Eunice sniffed. "She was the best friend in the world."

"You must have been very close. All those years together in the 'Otters'. Part of a winning team. It's a shame I didn't get the chance to know her better. I was just speaking to Reverend Cattermole, and Helen sounds like a formidable lady."

"She was that. So intelligent. I could sit and listen to her for hours on end."

"And such an outstanding athlete. 'Walkathon Champion' for seven years straight, that is an amazing achievement. I can understand why you were upset with her for leaving for the 'Strollers', but at least you ended as friends, eh?"

Eunice shifted awkwardly in her chair. "What makes you say that? You don't have the first idea about how we left it!"

"I'm sorry, it's just that I saw the two of you chatting by the tree outside the vicarage after the meeting. You seemed to be fast friends."

"That? Oh, yes. Well, she was so upset about the jam, you see. I was just telling her not to worry." Eunice snatched the serviette from my hand and wailed. "Helen and her bloody tarts!"

"Look, I'm sorry if I hit a nerve. Let's forget about dessert. I don't need the extra calories anyway. You've had a long day. Let's finish here, and you can go home and rest. Obviously, no hymns for the service, as she wasn't a believer, but did she have any favourite songs?"

Eunice's tears subsided long enough for us to map out a list of songs and a selection of suitable poems. It's amazing what you can find on Google. There was enough to be getting on with, and I could see that Eunice was struggling. I offered to liaise with Leo Peasbody on her behalf and sort out all the arrangements.

"All you have to do is to be there on the day. I will let you know when the coroner releases the body, and we can set a date. In the meantime, if you can draw up a list of people to invite, that would be great." Eunice nodded. "I imagine a lot of her students and colleagues from the university will want to show their respects. Perhaps Sonia would help get their contact details?"

Eunice's brow furrowed. "We don't need her help. I can handle it."

"Can I help you pack up? I've kept you back far too long."

"No, I would rather do it by myself, Vicar. I enjoy working when the shop is closed, and you have a ferry to catch."

"This is true. Well, if you think of anything else, just email me or drop me a text. I guess you'll change that display now, what with Keith in prison." I pointed to the fully stocked range of 'Hudson's Homemade'.

"Yes, I guess they will be more difficult to shift now." Eunice shrugged. "I'll see what Maureen says. Such a waste, though. We could just relabel."

"Yes, well. I'll leave you in peace." Walking back towards the exit, my phone rang. It was Zuzu. "Hi Sis, any news?" I waved back at Eunice to let her know I would be off as soon as I took this call and turned towards the barn door.

Zuzu sounded very excited. "Dave is very professional, isn't he? I had to promise all sorts to prise this out of him. Not that I'm complaining. I'm on the train to his house as we speak."

I didn't want to think about what she promised; it felt a tad unsavoury pimping out my sister for information. I needed to keep her on track. "And?"

I smiled back at Eunice. She didn't look too happy at my still hanging around. I guessed she was keen to shut up shop. I mimed the universal sign of being bored with a wave of my hand over my yawning mouth and whispered, "I'm sorry". I rooted around in my pocket for my scooter keys and pulled them out to show I was on my way, then moved closer to the door and back to the conversation.

My sister continued, "Oh. Yes. It's the jam. Must have been Keith for the lot. Very cunning if you ask me."

Zuzu's words confused me.

"It can't have been. Did the Inspector say what flavour jam?"

"Yes, a cake-themed one... Er?"

Without thinking, I blurted out, "Bakewell Tart?"

"Yes, that's it! How did you know?"

Suddenly, it all fell into place. When I had asked for an answer and saw that parade of faces, it didn't end with Keith. It included Eunice and then poor Helen. If I hadn't dismissed this all as nonsense, perhaps I could have saved her. Was it a premonition, or had the deed already happened?

I didn't have time to answer my sister or process any further. Eunice pushed ahead of me, blocking my path. "Give me the phone, Reverend Ward."

"Why did you kill her, Eunice? She was your friend?"

"Just give me the phone. I'm sorry. I really am. But I can't let you go."

Caged Animal

I could hear Zuzu's distant voice through the phone's speaker. "At least let me sign off, or she will worry." I pleaded with Eunice with my eyes, but hers were cold in reply. She snatched at my hand, I blocked her with my free arm but stumbled back. The scooter keys skidded under a crate of carrots. Eunice took advantage and wrestled me further into the food hall.

My hip caught on a table, sending a display of folk art kettles to the ground with an alarming clatter. I manoeuvred around, kicking some pots at my assailant. One hit her squarely in the shin. This gave me a few moments to put some distance between us. I needed a weapon, something to defend myself with. The butchery, maybe there were some knives there. I needed to act quickly. I picked up another of the kettles. With my left hand, I lobbed it at Eunice's forehead.

It missed, naturally, I can barely throw anything with my right arm let alone my left, but as Eunice dodged the metal projectile; I dashed to the meat counter. There was a wooden knife block with a gleaming array of potential weapons.

"Vicar, stay away from the knives. I will not hurt you. Promise. I panicked." Eunice pleaded.

I pulled out a six-inch stainless steel blade and walked back towards her. "Yeah, well, I'll keep this one close for my own peace of mind." I motioned with the knife for Eunice to take a seat. In the tussle, my call to Zuzu had dropped. I had no way of knowing how much she had heard of the last few minutes. "Sit down and put your hands on the table where I can see them." I wasn't sure what to do now. How do I call for help and keep the knife pointed at Eunice? There was no way I was letting my guard down. I pocketed the phone.

"Don't you want to know why?" Eunice sneered. I felt she was trying to brazen it out, but her demeanor was more akin to a petulant teenager.

"Because you loved her. You felt betrayed. You were angry she left the 'Otters', and you."

Eunice sniffed. Her lips trembled. "She left me for that silly little tart, Sonia. She was making a fool of herself. I tried to tell her. To reason with her."

"But Sonia is her student!" I was shocked. Sonia was over eighteen. They are consenting adults. Still, ethical or not, it wasn't an excuse for murder. "You were jealous."

"I was nothing without her. Nothing. Look at me! I know what people think. The frumpy old maid, no good for anything other than a few hours work in a poxy farm shop. No one appreciates what I do for the Rambler's Association. Maureen takes me for granted. Conrad hasn't even tried to proposition me! Do you know how redundant that makes you feel? He tries it on with anything in a skirt. Helen was a beacon. My inspiration. My life."

"Then why take hers? This wasn't an act of passion. You planned it. You hoped to hide it amongst all the other illnesses. When I called you said you were ill, but you lied, didn't you? You were already covering your tracks!"

Eunice reached into her pocket. Scared that she had a weapon, I banged on the table. "I was only getting a tissue," she said meekly as she produced the crumpled serviette I had given her earlier. "I was feeling unwell." Eunice looked down at her feet as she spoke. "I didn't lie to you. Just didn't tell Helen. Couldn't risk her not wanting to accept my gift, you see? I thought we could go together. I had already spread some on my toast, but I hadn't put it to my mouth." She looked up and stared at me, her eyes wide and obviously frightened. "When I saw how much pain she was in, it was terrifying. I chickened out."

"And you didn't call for help? You didn't even try to save her?"

"I held her." Eunice sobbed. "I cradled her in my arms. Didn't let go until she was cold. I told her I was sorry."

I thought to myself, 'Well, that's okay then', but such cynicism wasn't helpful. If I was going to get us out of this stand-off, I needed to make Eunice comfortable before handing her over to the police.

"I understand. You didn't want to lose her. You thought you would be together forever, and then along comes this university undergraduate who was everything you felt you weren't. Young, attractive, and clever. But you are clever. You worked all this out on your own. Tell me, how did you do it? How did you get the poison in the jam?"

"Oh, that was easy. There's a pestle and mortar behind you in the cupboard. Used it to grind up some cherry pit seeds. I didn't steal them! I paid for them. Just a punnet. I used a couple and took the rest home to make a pie. I have the receipt."

"I don't think Maureen will be angry with you for taking a few cherries, given the circumstances." I offered.

"No, I dare say, you're right." Eunice's grey face grew more shadowed. The full weight of her guilt was weighing heavily upon her. "I washed it thoroughly, too."

"Washed what? Oh, the pestle and mortar. Well, that's good. So that's how you made the cyanide?" I was softening. Eunice was scared, but I still needed to keep my guard up. As Frederico would say, there is nothing more dangerous than a caged animal.

"I knew it disappointed her not to get a jar of her favourite jam, and there are a dozen of them here." Eunice pointed over to the 'Hudson's Homemade' display. "So, I promised her I would bring a couple over. That's what you saw us talking about after the meeting. I said it was a peace offering, and it was, at the time."

"So, what happened?"

"Sonia happened." Eunice spat out her words like they were covered in venom. "On the ferry crossing. I saw her sidling up to Helen. She claimed she was too hot in that stupid blue sweater. She made sure Helen could see her taking it off. Some of her tee-shirt caught as she lifted it above her head. She was in no rush to protect her modesty. I knew what she was doing, the tart!"

"So, that's when you thought about the cyanide."

"Well, hearing about the other illnesses gave me the idea. I figured it was probably food poisoning. I didn't know it was the jam, that was just a freaky coincidence. Easy enough to open and reseal the jars."

"So I understand."

"The label came off a bit in the process, but I glued it back down as best I could. I told her it was going cheap because of the damage - she always liked a bargain. It was the only way to be sure she ate it in front of me."

"And you planned to join her."

"Yes. I should have died too!" Eunice kicked at the table, pushing the chair back violently. She leaped towards the display of 'Hudson's Homemade' and started frantically pulling off all the jars, sending them crashing to the floor. Splintered glass mixed with the sticky preserve, but she didn't notice or care. I was afraid Eunice was going to hurt herself.

"Hello there! Do you ladies need any assistance?"

Conrad! *Thank goodness!*

"Here! Be careful, Eunice is, er, upset."

"Well, looks to me like something's spooked her. I'm good at handling a frightened filly. Stand aside, Vicar. I say, why do you have a knife?"

Eunice lunged at Conrad. Initially taken off guard, he rallied quickly and wrapped his arms around her from behind as she tried to push past. Her legs kicked out as he lifted her off the ground. She even tried to bite him.

"Now, now, dear. No need for that. Let's get you on one of these here chairs, shall we?" Conrad carried Eunice back to the eating area. She was frantically wriggling every which way.

"I think I'm going to need a little help... Vicar?"

We needed to restrain her somehow. I needed to act quickly before Eunice got the better of my tweed-clad knight in shining armour.

"I'll see if there is any rope or something in the storeroom. Can you hold her for a bit?"

Conrad nodded. I ran back towards the room Eunice had emerged from earlier. There was a stack of cable ties and other bits of packing equipment, presumably to process food orders from the shop. I grabbed a few and returned as quickly as possible. With Conrad maintaining a firm hold, I used the cables to tie Eunice's hands and feet to the chair. Once secure, Conrad loosened his grip and took up a seat on the opposite side of the table. I sat beside him, finally putting the knife down between us.

"Now," Conrad propped himself up on the table as he caught his breath. "Which of you lovely ladies is going to tell me what the devil is going on here?"

"Conrad, you might want to grab yourself a cuppa. I need to call the police!"

The Winner Takes it All

L ady Arabella Somerstone-Wright stood before the assembled crowd. Her son Tristan proudly by her side, holding aloft the coveted 'Wesberrey Walkathon Cup'.

"It gives me immense pleasure to announce the winner of this year's walkathon, but before I do, we have a special announcement. I would like you to welcome on stage the chair of the Wesberrey Walkathon Committee and parish priest of our beloved St. Bridget's, Reverend Jessamy Ward!"

I walked carefully up the rickety steps to the side of the temporary podium, shook hands with Arabella, and took my place in front of the microphone. I was used to speaking from a pulpit, but I had never addressed a crowd as big as that which filled Market Square and Harbour Quay on this sublimely sunny Easter Saturday. When I trained to be an actress, all those years ago, I dreamed of commanding a stage like this, but the reality was terrifying.

I knew my lines. I had rehearsed them repeatedly with my niece Freya, who was visiting from university. Out in front, I could see my mother, and from where I stood, she genuinely seemed to beam with pride. My family stood around her. The 'Walkers' had gathered together next to the ice-cream van. Lenten vows completely forgotten for another year. The 'Otters' and the 'Strollers' grouped nearby, all keen to hear the results of the race.

"Ladies and gentlemen! The competition today has been a beautiful example of the wider community coming together. Today members of three walking groups from across the county have walked together in memory of one of our number who sadly is not here with us today. Professor Helen Linden was an avid rambler and a shining example to us all. She won this trophy for seven years in a row and undoubtedly would have won it for an eighth time today. It is, therefore, the decision of the committee to rename the walkathon in her honour. The winner of today's event will be the first recipient of the 'Helen Linden Memorial Cup'!"

The crowd erupted. Klaxons and horns blared. The sound booth pumped out "We are the champions" by Queen. I felt like I was in one of those teenage 'coming of age' movies; where the geeky girl is crowned prom queen and kisses the high school quarterback to the sound of a marching band. This wasn't Hollywood, though, and there was no prom queen. Whoever was to be the first winner of the 'Helen Linden Memorial Cup' would find their victory bittersweet.

I stepped aside. "Well done, Rev," whispered Arabella as she stepped forward. "I hate public speaking, don't you?" I saw her take a deep breath to calm her nerves.

"Thank you, Reverend Ward. It is my honour to announce that the inaugural winner of the 'Helen Linden Memorial Cup', gee, that is quite a mouthful, isn't it? Anyway... the winner is —" Arabella opened the envelope in her hand. "Frederico D'Souza, of the 'Wesberrey Walkers'!"

This time the crowd's response was not so wild. There were a few light-hearted boos from our rivals, but the acknowledged truth was that no one could compete with Frederico's level of fitness. The outcome was obvious from the start.

There was no need for the winner to make a speech, but that did not stop Frederico, who took the stage to make an announcement of his own.

"Senhoras e senhores! Thank you for your warm welcome and for the opportunity to compete for this magnificent cup. I never met Professor Linden, but I understand that she was a woman of grand passion. She had an unwavering commitment to her work and her students. I am proud to take on her spirit as I begin my new role at the University of

Stourchester. From next week, I will join the 'Stourchester Strollers' and I declare here and now. We will be back next year to defend my title as 'Walkathon Champion'!"

Unsurprisingly, the Wesberrey 'burros', and my sister cheered at the news. Hopefully, Frederico would find happiness in the big city.

Arabella went to take the microphone back, but Frederico raised his hand. He had to make another announcement. My heart sank. Surely he would not embarrass himself and my sister in public like this? Not now, not today.

"Mais uma coisa por favor. Please, one more thing." He waved at the sound booth and gave the DJ a nod. The theme tune from Franco Zeffirelli's 'Romeo and Juliet', a.k.a 'A time for us' poured from the PA system. Oh my goodness, he *was* going to embarrass us all! I couldn't look. I tried not to listen. Then I heard a familiar voice talking over the fading music.

"Is this thing workin'? Barbara? Barbara Graham. Ah, there you are."

Phil?

"Barbara, maybe we're a bit too old for all this, but... you see, a few weeks ago, I thought I was going to lose you." The crowd pushed a blushing parish secretary to the front of the stage. "Since then, I 'aven't been able to think about anything other than how I missed your smile. I know we see each other every day around St. Bridget's, but that is no longer enough. It never has been. The thought of you not being in my life is, well, it's impossible. That's what it is. Miss Graham..." Phil took the microphone from the stand and lowered himself down on one knee.

"Oh Phil, you silly old fool, how are you going to get back up?" Barbara flapped her hands and laughed.

Unperturbed, he continued, "Miss Barbara Graham, will you do me the 'onour of agreeing to be my wife?"

Barbara, all blissfully giggling and as pink as the flamingo earrings that dangled from her ears, placed her hands on her heart and answered.

"Oh, Mr Vickers, I thought you'd never ask!"

A stray voice from the assembled crowd called out, "About bleedin' time!"

Phil dropped the microphone and to an ear-piercing serenade of audio feedback and cheers, he jumped off the stage. Barbara rushed forward to catch him and, in true Hollywood style, they hugged.

St. Bridget's prince and princess were finally going to tie the knot. It would be the wedding of the year, no doubt about it.

Wesberrey, my new home, was always full of surprises.

What's Next for Reverend Jess?

DIVINE DEATH

Things appear to be settling down in the island parish of St. Bridget's, and Rev Jess Ward is enjoying the relative peace in the lead up to Pentecost. So, maybe it's unwise to invite in the local archaeological society to dig up the old well?

What will the dig beneath the floor of the baptismal font uncover?

Spring is a time of fresh starts and new beginnings. Is that romance we smell in the air?

Life is skipping along until a sudden death takes the spring out of Jess's step.

Old rivalries, deception and ambition are all viable motives for violence, but could it be a crime of passion, or even self-defence?

In a mystery that appears to involve some of her closest family and friends, Jess turns to her ancient past to help solve this latest tragedy.

Divine Death is the fourth book in the Isle of Wesberrey Series by Penelope Cress.

About the Author

P enelope lives on an island off the coast of Kent, England, with her four children and an elderly Jack Russell Terrier. A lover of murder mystery and cups of tea (served with a stack of digestive biscuits), she writes quaint cosy mysteries and other feel-good stories from a corner table in the vintage tea shop on the high street. Penelope loves nostalgia and all things retro. Her taste in music is also very last century.

Find out more about Penelope at

Acknowledgements

This book would never have been finished without the incredible support of a bunch of awesome female writers called the Coronitas. These amazing women kept me focused and sane during the early months of the Corona lockdown.

Thank you ladies. I am honoured to be in your tribe. I have learnt so much about writing, the craft and the business, from you.

A huge thanks to the organisers of 20Books Edinburgh where I met the Coronitas in July 2019. It was the most amazing writers conference and retreat and seriously life changing. Craig and Michael, I am forever in your debt.

It was also in Edinburgh that I met my talented cover designer, Mariah, who agreed to design these beautiful covers for me, even though her order book was already full to the brim.

I want to thank my children and my friends who have supported me along this journey.

I need to give a particular shout out to my work colleagues for not laughing when I said I wanted to do this. Especially to Caroline, who volunteered to read my first book when it was in its first draft and has cheered me on ever since. It was Caroline who came up with the name for the new cafe - Dungeons and Vegans. Pure genius!

And last, but not least, I want to thank you for reading my little story. I hope that the people of Wesberrey have warmed your heart.

If you would like to know more about Jess's childhood, you can get a free story called Jubilee Jinks by signing up to my newsletter at .

It's set in 1977, a year I remember all too well. My late mother was a huge fan of the Royal Family and we stood for hours on the roadside by Clapham Common to see Her Majesty, The Queen whizzed past in her state limousine. This short story, like much of this series is inspired by my mother and I feel that she is beside me as I write.

I would love to hear what you think about my favourite place to escape to. Please email me at penelope@penelopecresss.com

Want to know more?

Greenfield press is the brainchild of bestselling author Steve Higgs. He specializes in writing fast paced adventurous mystery and urban fantasy with a humorous lilt. Having made his money publishing his own work, Steve went looking for a few 'special' authors whose work he believed in.

Georgia Wagner was the first of those, but to find out more and to be the first to hear about new releases and what is coming next, you can join the Facebook group by copying the following link into your browser - www.facebook.com/GreenfieldPress.

More Books By Steve Higgs

Blue Moon Investigations
Paranormal Nonsense
The Phantom of Barker Mill
Amanda Harper Paranormal Detective
The Klowns of Kent
Dead Pirates of Cawsand
In the Doodoo With Voodoo
The Witches of East Malling
Crop Circles, Cows and Crazy Aliens
Whispers in the Rigging
Bloodlust Blonde – a short story
Paws of the Yeti
Under a Blue Moon – A Paranormal
Detective Origin Story
Night Work
Lord Hale's Monster
The Herne Bay Howlers
Undead Incorporated
The Ghoul of Christmas Past
The Sandman
Jailhouse Golem
Shadow in the Mine
Ghost Writer

Felicity Philips Investigates
To Love and to Perish
Tying the Noose
Aisle Kill Him
A Dress to Die For
Wedding Ceremony Woes

Patricia Fisher Cruise Mysteries
The Missing Sapphire of Zangrabar
The Kidnapped Bride
The Director's Cut
The Couple in Cabin 2124
Doctor Death
Murder on the Dancefloor
Mission for the Maharaja
A Sleuth and her Dachshund in Athens
The Maltese Parrot
No Place Like Home

Patricia Fisher Mystery Adventures
What Sam Knew
Solstice Goat
Recipe for Murder
A Banshee and a Bookshop
Diamonds, Dinner Jackets, and Death
Frozen Vengeance
Mug Shot
The Godmother
Murder is an Artform
Wonderful Weddings and Deadly
Divorces
Dangerous Creatures

Patricia Fisher: Ship's Detective Series
The Ship's Detective
Fitness Can Kill
Death by Pirates
First Dig Two Graves

Albert Smith Culinary Capers
Pork Pie Pandemonium
Bakewell Tart Bludgeoning
Stilton Slaughter
Bedfordshire Clanger Calamity
Death of a Yorkshire Pudding
Cumberland Sausage Shocker
Arbroath Smokie Slaying
Dundee Cake Dispatch
Lancashire Hotpot Peril
Blackpool Rock Bloodshed
Kent Coast Oyster Obliteration
Eton Mess Massacre
Cornish Pasty Conspiracy

Realm of False Gods
Untethered magic
Unleashed Magic
Early Shift
Damaged but Powerful
Demon Bound
Familiar Territory
The Armour of God
Live and Die by Magic
Terrible Secrets

Printed in Great Britain
by Amazon

21168857R00092